MAYHEM AT MAGNOLIA MANOR

HOLLY MOULDER

Bladensburg, MD

❧Inscript

Published by Inscript Books
a division of Dove Christian Publishers
P.O. Box 611
Bladensburg, MD 20710-0611
www.inscriptpublishing.com

Book Design by Mark Yearnings
ISBN: 978-1-7375177-4-0
Library of Congress Control No. 2021950697
Copyright © 2021 by Holly Moulder

Printed in the United States of America

In loving memory of my mom, Anne B. Fisher

The Lord shall preserve thy going out and thy coming in from this time forth, and even for evermore. Psalm 121: 8

Cast of Characters

Marjorie Sims: Also known as Marjorie Riley, she is a 62-year-old accountant from Philadelphia. Late one night, Marjorie witnesses the kidnapping of a Philadelphia police detective who is later found murdered. Marjorie is quickly placed in protective custody by the U.S. Marshals who want her to testify against Kingpin, the boss of an organized crime syndicate.

Stephen Breckinridge: A U.S. Marshal with training in physical therapy, Stephen accompanies Marjorie to her new home where he serves as her bodyguard against Kingpin's men.

Edna Duncan: The elderly widow of James, a Baptist minister. Edna works with Stephen to help protect Marjorie.

Beanie Buffala: Elderly widow of trucker Stan, and mother of five adult children. Beanie passes her days at the Magnolia Manor by solving mysteries with Edna.

Director William Peabody-Jones: Also known as PBJ. The director is a retired FBI agent who has been friends with Stephen for years. Although he always appears frumpy and unkempt, there's more to William than meets the eye.

Brett Hopewell: The new chaplain at Magnolia Manor, Pastor Hopewell claims to be born and bred in the Atlanta area. His handsome face and whiskey-smooth voice make the ladies of the Manor blush.

Pearl Porter: Pearl is the Manor's much-loved chef. Her salmon patties are literally to die for. After work hours, Pearl is responsible for taking care of her aging mother, Velma. But Pearl has a terrible secret that she can't share with anyone.

Irene Spencer: An elderly resident at the Manor, Irene is the proud owner of a miscreant cat, Mr. Whiskers. Irene complains constantly to anyone who will listen, especially PBJ. Irene's mission is to get Edna and Beanie kicked out of the Manor — for good.

Charlie Richardson: Edna's high school sweetheart, rumor has it Charlie once worked at NASA. Or did he? But now he's living at the Manor, receiving care for Alzheimer's disease.

MAYHEM
AT
MAGNOLIA MANOR

One

A Terrifying Elevator Ride

*M*arjorie Sims despised the elevator in the Broad Street parking garage. With its stained walls, cracked linoleum floor, and 70s-era Muzak tunes playing nonstop, it was the perfect setting for a murder. The dim overhead lights blinked on and off in a scary serial-killer kind of way. The air smelled like Old Spice and old sweat, an odor that made Marjorie gag every time she stepped through the doors. To make matters even worse, the ancient machinery that hoisted this death box between floors creaked louder than an old man's knees.

It felt like a scene straight from a Stephen King novel. All that it needed was a bloody knife stuck in the wall and a dead body splayed across the floor.

Didn't help that Marjorie had a touch of claustrophobia, a fear of closed-in places she could trace back to when Mikey Mahoney, her childhood bully, locked her in the tiny storage shed behind her Pennsylvania home. The shed was full of spider webs and dead bugs and was so small she couldn't stand up. She beat and beat on the door. With tears streaming down her face, she screamed to be let out.

But all she heard was Mikey's cruel laughter.

After what seemed like hours to an eight-year-old, Mikey's sister Kimberly finally let her out.

But Marjorie never forgot the feeling of being trapped in that box. The panic. The terror. And now, closed-in places like this elevator sent her stress levels into the stratosphere.

And unless she arrived at work at the crack of dawn, she really had no choice but to ride it twice a day. The accounting firm she worked for, one of the most prestigious in Philadelphia, rented the entire deck for its employees to use. Parking in Philly was notoriously hard to find, so a private parking deck was a coveted perk. And when Marjorie could get there early, like before seven in the morning, she landed a spot on the first floor. No elevator needed.

But today, she was late. An overnight ice storm had left traffic on the Schuylkill Expressway backed up for miles. So, the search for a spot led her to the eighth floor.

Then, to make up for that late start that morning, Marjorie had worked well past her usual six o'clock quitting time. Tax season was just starting, but her bosses were already in a frenzy. She figured a few extra hours would help her get a handle on the chaos.

Now, alone on the first floor of the parking deck, she tapped her foot impatiently as she waited for the death box to lumber its way down. She checked her watch. Midnight, on the dot. The classic time for murder and mayhem. *Great, just great.*

She'd celebrate birthday number sixty-two in just two

weeks. Maybe it was time to think about retirement. Snag that social security check and crack open that pension nest egg. After all, forty years of dedicated service to Bradley and Bradley Accounting seemed like more than enough. With no family to speak of, she could travel the world. Settle on whatever beach grabbed her fancy.

And then there'd be no more elevators, no more traffic. Ah, *paradise.*

Standing in the elevator, Marjorie took a deep breath of sort-of-fresh parking garage air as she pushed the button for the eighth floor. But just before the doors thudded shut, a man rushed on.

From the corner of her eye, Marjorie gave him the once over, trying to decide if he was dangerous. Tall, late forties. Brown raincoat, and a battered black fedora pulled down over his face.

Who wears fedoras anymore? she wondered. *Certainly not accountants. Old police detectives, maybe?*

Fedora-man pushed the button for the seventh floor and then took a step back from the elevator doors. His raincoat shifted. *Was that a revolver-shaped lump in his coat, or is my imagination running off the rails again?*

She shook her head and sighed. *I've got to stop bingeing on those Hallmark Channel mysteries.*

Still, there was just something strange about this guy. To fend off her rising panic, Marjorie ran through all the steps she'd learned at her Safety for Seniors class last month. Look confident and stand up straight. Don't slouch like a victim. She lifted her chin, threw back her shoulders. Stretched out her five-foot-six-inch frame.

Darn. Should have worn high heels today. Could have added a couple inches.

Marjorie pulled the belt of her black leather coat tighter around her waist. She fingered the car keys already in her pocket. She grabbed the pink plastic case of the MaceFace pepper spray attached to her keychain, her finger ready to hit the magic button. Richie, the self-defense guru who'd taught the class at the senior center, had warned against carrying the small canister, explaining that the stuff could end up being used against them. Or, it could blow back in their faces, get on their clothes, put them at risk. He favored stabbing assailants in the eye with car keys instead.

Marjorie shuddered. She didn't think she could ever stab someone in the eye. But who knows? In a pinch, maybe she could. And maybe this was just that kind of pinch.

So, she'd bought the pepper spray anyway, against Richie's advice. And now it was tucked in her pocket, ready for action. Marjorie's cellphone was in the other pocket, ready to dial 911. Her purse strap was wrapped securely around her body.

An assailant would have to cut it off her cold, dead body. Happy thought.

She felt prepared. Sort of.

The man jiggled the coins in his pants pocket and rocked back and forth on his well-worn heels. The floor numbers slowly climbed. 2. 3. 4. He studied the panel and let out an impatient sigh as the rickety box shimmied and shook its way from floor to floor.

The stranger glanced at Marjorie and smiled. Seemed like a kind smile, and Marjorie let down her guard just a little. Maybe he wasn't a threat after all. And he had nice eyes. Be a shame to stick a car key in them.

A sudden burst of brilliance overhead, a loud *POP* from the ceiling, and the lights went out. And to Marjorie's dismay, nothing's quite as terrifyingly pitch black as a parking garage elevator at midnight.

The stranger came to the rescue. He pulled out his cellphone and turned on the flashlight app. "How did we ever manage without these things?" he asked.

Marjorie smiled, grateful for the light.

She breathed a sigh of relief when the elevator shuddered to a stop on the seventh floor. She'd ride up one more floor, by herself this time, hurry to her trusty Camry, and drive away into the night. Pour herself a nice glass of Merlot when she got home. A bubble bath. Safe and sound.

At least, that was her plan until the doors slowly opened on the seventh floor. When the stranger stepped out, two thugs dressed in hooded sweatshirts and fancy tennis shoes appeared out of the shadows. They grabbed fedora-man and dragged him toward a waiting sedan. As Marjorie watched in terror, the man's raincoat opened wide, revealing a gun — and a badge. He was a cop!

The fedora-man yelled one word at Marjorie.

"Kingpin!"

The two men tried to jam the policeman into the back of the car, but he wasn't going down easy. He slugged one of the men in the jaw, sending him sprawling to the solid concrete deck. But the other man shoved a gun in the cop's back and pushed him into the car's rear seat.

The driver's side door opened, and a man got out. He was at least six feet tall, 300 pounds. Terrifyingly big. A defensive end for the Philadelphia Eagles would have been intimidated by this guy.

The parking garage light helped Marjorie get a pretty good look at the driver's face. His eyes were steely blue. A jagged scar ran along his cheek. His salt and pepper hair was pulled back in a shoulder-length ponytail, and he wore a beat-up Phillies cap on his head. Fury radiated from every pore on his acne-scarred face, and he was coming straight at Marjorie with his gun drawn.

He shot one time into the dark elevator. The bullet ricocheted off the dull gray wall before penetrating the metal inches above Marjorie's head. Just like in the movies, she actually heard the bullet whizz by.

Panicked, Marjorie hit the floor. She pulled the pepper spray from her pocket, and without taking the time to aim, shot blindly at the open elevator door.

Bullseye.

Maybe there's a God after all. Marjorie couldn't believe it. The assailant yelped in pain, covered his face with his hands, and backed away from the door. One of the hooded thugs grabbed his arm and dragged him back to the sedan, put him in the back seat, and got in on the driver's side.

Trembling, she reached up and pushed the button, closing the elevator doors.

She was thrown back into pitch-black darkness. Thank goodness.

She heard the sedan's tires scream as it took off down the ramp and out of the garage.

She had the presence of mind to turn on her phone. The soft glow helped her locate number eight on the panel. When she got to her floor, Marjorie burst out of the elevator, hit unlock on her key fob, and ran as fast as her trembling legs would carry her toward the safety of that *beep beep.* She struggled to open the door but finally made it inside her car. She jammed the key in the ignition, started the engine, and careened down the ramp to the exit. Her tires shrieked as she dialed 911.

The exit gate lay in pieces on the asphalt, a souvenir left by the bad guys as they crashed through on their way out. She didn't stop to look both ways like her mother had taught her. She just drove like a crazy woman into the middle of Broad Street, briefly sending up a prayer of thanks that no one else was on the road at this time of night. Well, except for kidnappers and murderers.

Marjorie arrived home at record speed. She watched in the rear-view mirror all the way, just waiting for the bad guys to come up behind her and run her off the road or shoot out her windows. This was no Hallmark movie. This was for real, and she was terrified.

The garage door took forever to go up, but at last, she was able to pull in, turn off her car, and race to the safety of her own home.

The two officers were hesitant to believe her story. An older woman, fending off an attack with a pink canister of MaceFace? And the bit about the police detective being kidnapped? It just didn't make sense.

Marjorie poured herself another glass of wine, just to calm her nerves, and explained the evening's events again to the unconvinced officers. How she'd worked late, ridden the elevator with the stranger — who was probably a police detective — and then avoided being shot by fighting back with the only weapon she had on hand — MaceFace.

When Marjorie had finished her tale the second time, the police officers shook their heads in disbelief. They decided to take her to police headquarters downtown and let her tell her story to the detectives. Maybe they could clear this all up.

One thing was for sure. This woman had been through a

terrible ordeal. She couldn't stop shaking. The officers took her arms and gently helped her into the police car.

A few minutes later, she was sitting at the police station, sipping hot tea and looking through mugshots. Until she found him. The man who shot at her in the parking deck. The startled detective looked at her, shock written on his face.

And maybe something akin to admiration?

"This is the man who tried to shoot you?" he asked. Hearing the excitement in his voice, a group of officers gathered around to see what was going on.

"Yes, that's him. Who is he?" Marjorie asked.

"That's Kingpin. He controls all the drug trafficking in south Philly. The detective you saw dragged into the car had been investigating him for months. Your testimony may be enough to put him away for good." The officer shook his head. "You're lucky to be alive, lady. Kingpin doesn't usually miss his targets."

And that's how Marjorie's years of elevator riding came to an end. But pretty soon, she'd recall that time as the days of wine and roses. There were no white sand beaches or exotic umbrella drinks in her future. In fact, compared to the nightmare she was about to face, a scary elevator ride was a walk in the park.

MAGNOLIA
MANOR

Two

A New Life

"*I*t's time to go, Marjorie." U.S. Marshal Stephen Breckinridge slung a canvas bag over his shoulder and closed his bedroom door. Marjorie took a quick look around her room, checking for any items she might have missed. She zipped up her small suitcase and followed Stephen down the stairs.

Knock, knock. Pause. Knock, knock, knock.

Marjorie recognized the signal. The marshals used it to let each other know it was safe to open the door.

"Go straight to the van and get in," he said. "One of the drivers will take your suitcase for you. Don't look around. Don't speak to anyone. Got it?"

Marjorie nodded grimly at the man, her nearly constant companion since the U.S. Marshals paid her that first visit. Right after Kingpin had nearly killed her.

They had brought her to this house the very night she'd

identified Kingpin as the elevator shooter. From the very beginning, Stephen had done his best to make her feel safe. He'd cooked their meals, played cards with her—anything to distract her. They tried to watch TV together, but it was tough to find a channel they both liked. Marjorie loved the Hallmark channel, and Stephen was a news junkie. Still, they worked it out and soon developed a friendship.

Not that she hadn't noticed that Stephen was a very attractive man. With thick silver hair and ice-blue eyes, he was a real looker. In his early sixties, like Marjorie, he still had a nice, trim physique. But the show-stopper? A smile that showed off dimples, perfectly straight white teeth, and little crinkles around those gorgeous eyes.

But when it came down to it, the only thing that really mattered to Marjorie was that she knew she could trust this man, no matter what.

Stephen opened the front door, and Marjorie hurried down the concrete steps into the bright sunlight. Keeping her head down, she walked quickly to the van, just as she had been told. She climbed inside and slid across the vinyl seat. Stephen buckled in beside her, and the van door slammed shut.

Marjorie was headed to the WITSEC center, a secret facility outside Washington, D.C., designed to prepare protected witnesses for their new lives.

Here she'd get her new name, new documents, even a new Social Security number. She'd learn about her new community, somewhere in Georgia. Far away from the dangers in Philadelphia. She could never go back there again.

She'd made the decision to give up her home, her friends, everything that was familiar to her. All because of what she had seen and heard in that parking garage on Broad Street.

"How far is this place?" Marjorie asked. She chewed on her lower lip, a nervous habit she'd had ever since she was a little girl. It bothered her that she couldn't see outside. Claustrophobia struck again. The windows in the van had been blacked out, making her feel like the walls were closing in. There was even a wall between the drivers and passengers so that no one riding in the back could see the road ahead.

She shoved her hands into her pockets and burrowed down in her thick sweater. She closed her eyes and took a deep breath.

"C'mon, Marjorie. You know the rules. I can't tell you that." Stephen squeezed her hand through her sweater pocket. He knew Marjorie was scared to death, and she had good reason. Robert King, the criminal who called himself the Kingpin, was a terrifying man. His reputation for violence and cruelty was well known in the law enforcement community.

Kingpin controlled a legion of loyal followers — petty criminals and drug pushers hoping to make it big as part of Kingpin's organization — all of whom were now searching for Marjorie. Their aim was to silence her because of what she'd seen: the kidnapping of a Philadelphia detective whose body had been discovered on the banks of the Schuylkill River the very next day. It was a murder that could bring down Kingpin's empire.

As a witness to the kidnapping, Marjorie was Kingpin's number one target. So, the U.S. Marshals Service had stepped in to keep her safe until she could testify in court.

But Kingpin was on the run, and Marjorie was in extreme danger.

She glanced at Stephen, sitting silently beside her in the van. She watched him making notes on papers that were probably about her. But he couldn't share any of the information. She laid her head against the back of the seat and fell into a restless sleep.

Marjorie dreamed of her parents for the first time in years. They were beckoning to her, calling her to come to them. It was a bewildering dream, not comforting at all, and she woke up in a cold sweat when Stephen gently nudged her arm.

"We're here, Marjorie," he said softly. He slid the door open and jumped out, then turned back to offer his hand to Marjorie. "Welcome to WITSEC."

They had parked in an underground garage at the Safesite and Orientation Center for the Witness Security Program, better known as WITSEC. Marjorie followed Stephen into an elevator — this one a little better than the death box, but not much. They traveled up several floors before the doors opened onto a carpeted hallway.

Marjorie glanced up and down the hall. Bad lighting, stained carpeting. Beige, beige, and more beige. Faded artificial flowers on a side table did their best to welcome visitors, but the effect was more depressing than cheery.

They passed several rooms along the way, but the place was silent as stone. No TV noise, no music blaring through the walls, no children laughing.

"Are there other people here like me?" Marjorie asked as Stephen unlocked her door.

"Not allowed to tell you that. If there are other 'guests,' you won't see them. Everything here is very private, very self-contained. You'll eat all your meals in your room." Stephen rolled her suitcase into the room and flipped on the light.

"Home sweet home."

The walls and carpeting of the tiny room were the same dull beige color as the hallway. Apparently, the U.S. Marshals

Service did not intend to waste precious tax dollars on elaborate decor.

But at least the room was clean, and it contained everything she'd need for her short stay: a single bed, a well-worn sofa, and a dining table with two chairs. A dresser and mirror were pushed up against the wall next to a narrow closet. A coffee pot and microwave had been set up on a laminate counter close to a dorm-sized fridge. A door led to her private bathroom. A single rectangular window, placed high above the dresser, was narrow and tinted. Only the barest amount of sunlight passed through. It would be impossible to see outside without the help of a step stool.

"I'll be back in an hour," Stephen said, "and then we'll get to work. The quicker we get this done, the faster you get to your new home." His face turned serious. "Make sure you lock the door behind me."

After Stephen left, Marjorie unpacked the few things she'd brought with her. She'd been told that the Marshal's Service would provide some clothing for her, things that would be appropriate for her new location in Georgia. And, as promised, the tiny closet was already filled with new garments that were just her size. From the looks of the designer labels, the Marshal's Service had good shoppers. So, this was where they spent their money.

Marjorie pulled a lightweight gray sweater from the closet and found a pair of jeans in the dresser. She laid her clothes on the bed, grabbed her toiletry bag from the suitcase, and headed into the bathroom.

She was arranging her cosmetics on the vanity when she caught a glimpse of herself in the mirror. She was shocked by what she saw. A sixty-two-year-old woman with bags under her bloodshot eyes and deep lines around her mouth. Out-of-control brown hair streaked with gray, in desperate need of a good cut and professional color.

She looked awful.

And then she laughed out loud at the woman in the mirror. *Here you are in a government safe house, being chased by a brutal criminal, and you're worried about a little gray in your hair?* With a grin, she turned the shower on full blast and climbed in. The hot water instantly calmed her nerves and lifted her spirits.

Stephen knocked on her door in an hour, just as he promised. He had changed out of his suit into a pair of jeans and a Penn State sweatshirt. Marjorie couldn't help but admire how well he filled out his clothes. And those bright blue eyes gave her a little thrill each time he looked at her.

If she hadn't been fighting for her life, there might have been something there. But right now, there was no time for foolish romantic notions.

They sat at the little table in Marjorie's room and filled out paperwork for all the new documents she'd need to start her new life.

And then Stephen slid a DVD into his computer and brought up a video of what would soon be Marjorie's new home, Magnolia Manor in Palmetto, Georgia. "A retirement home for active seniors age fifty-five and up in a quiet little community just south of the bustling city of Atlanta," boasted the youngish-sounding narrator.

The video began with an overview of a stereotypical southern town. Palmetto's main street — actually named "Main Street" — was lined with old-fashioned storefronts that dated back to the early 1900s. Hanging baskets overflowing with bright red geraniums hung from vintage light poles that dotted the sidewalks. At one end of Main Street stood the Bank of Palmetto, a solid gray structure that inspired confidence and security. At the other end, hungry residents could complete their weekly grocery shopping at a modern-looking supermarket.

And running parallel to Main Street was a railroad. It had been used as far back as the Civil War, announced the narrator proudly, and was still used today to ship goods up and down the eastern seaboard. A quaint but deserted depot stood nearby, a reminder of times past when train travel was king.

Small roads ran under the railroad tracks, making use of overpasses and low bridges that had served the community for years. These roads led to Palmetto's suburbs, neighborhoods full of well-built but not high-priced family homes.

The video showed groups of happy, chatting residents of all ages seated at charming, open-air restaurants and cafes. Smiling children rode bikes, jumped rope, and licked ice cream cones on warm summer days. An idyllic little town.

She could almost hear the church bells ringing.

Andy and Barney should be driving down Main Street at any moment.

Compared to the towering, soot-covered snowbanks and freezing weather she'd left behind in Philadelphia, this place looked like Nirvana in the springtime.

It's almost too good to be true. And how would I fit in?

Aside from peaches and peanuts, Marjorie knew precious little about Georgia. But Stephen told her not to worry.

"Your cover story has you coming from Kansas, so we'll have you do a little reading about that. Just tell everyone you picked Georgia because of its warm climate and friendly people."

By the time they got to the end of the video, Marjorie was ready to pack her bags and head south.

Stephen gave her some important advice. "Remember, when you're asked questions about your past, just keep your answers very simple. You're a retired math teacher from Topeka. Don't give too much information. It's easy to get trapped into saying the wrong thing," Stephen warned. "Keep your answers short and sweet, and you'll do just fine. And I'll be there to help."

"You're going undercover, too?" Marjorie asked.

"Yes. Before I joined the Marshals Service, I was training to be a physical therapist. Got recruited right out of college. I'll use that knowledge as a cover at the retirement home. Shouldn't be too bad, helping little old ladies with bad knees and golfers with sore elbows."

"Sounds pretty awful if you want to know the truth, Stephen," Marjorie grimaced. "So, I'm supposed to be from Kansas, and everything about me is changed. Except I'm keeping my real first name? How come?" Marjorie asked.

Everything else about my life had been wiped clean. Why not my name, too?

"WITSEC found that people in hiding come off as more believable if they introduce themselves using their actual first name," he explained. "You can say it without thinking. Gives you some time to remember your fake last name." Stephen's expression was very serious. "Think of it as the little pause that can save your life."

The next three days flew by. Marjorie learned all she could about her new identity as she and Stephen reviewed everything she'd need to know. Her make-believe children's names, her past profession, her hobbies and interests.

Anything to make her lies believable.

In the evening, Marjorie read everything she could about Kansas. Major cities, the state bird and state song, local politicians. The list seemed endless. But she knew this information might just save her life, so she studied until she thought her brain couldn't hold one more sunflower-filled fact.

One afternoon, Stephen caught her singing, "I'm as corny as Kansas in autumn, high as a kite on the fourth of July."

"Well, that's a happy little tune," he said. "Make that one up yourself?"

Marjorie's jaw dropped. "You're kidding, right? It's from the musical South Pacific. You know, 'Gonna wash that man right out of my hair.'" Marjorie sang the lyrics, snapping her fingers and doing a little dance.

Stephen stared at her blankly.

Marjorie tried again. "Some enchanted evening, you will meet a stranger?" Crickets. "Sorry," he said.

"Oh, Stephen. We must do something about your musical theater education. When we get to Georgia, I'm going to get some DVDs, pop some popcorn, and introduce you to Rodgers and Hammerstein, or maybe Lerner and Lowe. It'll be awesome."

Stephen looked glum. "Can't wait."

On the morning of the fourth day, Stephen appeared at her door with a smile on his face and a stranger by his side. "Your reward for working so hard," he grinned. "Sharon's here to give you the full treatment. Time to wash that gray right out of your hair, right?"

Marjorie smiled broadly and threw her arms around Stephen's neck.

Within a couple of hours, a brand-new, updated Marjorie stared back at her from the bathroom mirror. Marjorie Simms was gone. And in her place was the new — and vastly improved — Marjorie Riley.

That afternoon, with Stephen by her side, Marjorie boarded

a plane that would whisk her to her new life in a little town in Georgia.

Three

Beanie and Edna, Crime Stoppers

"*H*ere she comes," Beanie whispered to Edna as she peered around the potted plant in the hall. "Get ready."

"Ready," Edna replied, raising her cane over her head. "Let's put an end to this crime spree once and for all."

"What are you going to do with that?" Beanie asked, her eyes wide. "Irene is eighty-eight. I don't think you're going to have to take her down with your bedazzled cane. Besides, that thing's getting glitter all over the floor."

Edna looked down at the little shiny pile on the gray carpet.

She smiled. "I know, but isn't it adorable? Rebecca said I should have a sparkly cane because it matches my personality. She's such a doll."

"Your granddaughter is precious," Beanie agreed, "but we've got to catch a crook right now. Try to stay focused."

Irene wobbled down the hall, her hands keeping a death grip

on the walker's rubber handles. She ran out of steam halfway to her room, so she plopped herself down on the walker's plushy seat to rest.

Beanie let out a low whistle. "Wow. Check it out. That Walk'n Roll 8000 is sharp. Just like the ad on TV. Adjustable seat, easy-glide wheels. A sturdy leatherette saddlebag on the front. And that shiny red paint job is the cat's meow.

Maybe I need to get my kids to order one of them for me from Amazon."

"Don't be ridiculous. You don't need one of those yet. You're the only one in the whole place who can still bend over to tie her shoes." Edna tapped her cane impatiently, releasing a cloud of glitter into the air. "This is taking too long. I'm missing the beginning of *Murder She Wrote*. What's she doing now?"

"She's checking her pulse. Hold on."

"Has she got that weirdo cat with her?" Edna whispered. "That animal gives me the creeps. One blue eye, one green eye. Stares a hole right through me. And did you notice the thing never blinks? Could star in its own horror movie."

"Wait," Beanie said, ignoring her friend's cat terror. "Irene's on the move. Get ready."

Irene stopped in front of her room, number 106. She slipped a key out of her dress pocket and unlocked her door. Leaving the Walk'n Roll 8000 parked in the hall, she tottered into her room, giving Mr. Whiskers time to stick his head out into the hall. He immediately spied Edna and glared at her.

"Come, come, Mr. Whiskers," Irene coaxed her cat. "Mama brought you some goodies from the dining room." Mr. Whiskers pulled his head back into the room, but not before he hissed at Edna.

"Did you hear that?" Edna whispered at Beanie. "And did

you see the evil eye he gave me? That cat is demon-possessed, no doubt about it."

"Well, he doesn't like you, that's for sure. But he's just a harmless ball of white fluff. Forget about him. Remember, we've got a job to do, Edna. Let's roll."

Edna and Beanie crept down the hall to Irene's room as quietly as their creaky bones would allow.

"Hand me the magnifying glass, Edna." Stooping down, Beanie examined the walker's undercarriage for identifying marks. "There it is," she whispered. "The telltale mark. Flo's initials: FE for Florence Emerson. Right where she said her son put them. Smart boy. He must have heard about Irene's penchant for 'borrowing' things — like shiny red Walk'n Roll 8000s."

As Edna helped Beanie to her feet, she said, "I'll go get Irene's real walker. You take Flo's to the game room. Flo said the pinochle club was playing in there this morning. She and Phyllis made the finals."

"I'm on it." Beanie scurried down the hall, the walker flashing a brilliant red in the morning light.

Edna hurried back to their hiding place and pulled Irene's walker out from behind the potted palm. It was no Walk'n Roll 8000, for sure. The wheels squeaked, and the red paint was chipped. It was dotted with dents where Irene had banged into walls — her driving was notoriously bad. The vinyl seat was cracked, and the leatherette saddlebag was MIA.

She pushed it to Irene's door and parked it where the Walk'n Roll had been. The theme from "Murder She Wrote" blared on the other side of the wall. Edna looked around for busybodies peeking out doorways.

Ha! No witnesses! Smiling, Edna hurried away from the

crime scene, her cane briskly thump-thumping down the hall.

Edna smiled triumphantly. *Another crime spree nipped in the bud by Edna and Beanie, detectives extraordinaire. But wouldn't it be great if we had a real mystery to solve?*

Although it seemed as if they'd been friends forever, Beanie and Edna had met about five years ago when Beanie moved into Magnolia Manor. She'd been newly widowed, her husband Stan having passed away a scant six months earlier. Edna, a widow herself, had been Beanie's rock. For the first year Beanie lived at the Manor, she and Edna had read the Bible every morning, mostly Psalms, and prayed together each night. And stone by stone, they'd built the kind of friendship that would last forever.

They realized early on in their friendship they both had an affinity for detective stories. The pair loved nothing better than solving a good mystery.

By lunchtime, news of the return of Florence's Walk'n Roll had spread through Magnolia Manor faster than a fresh whiff of Bengay. The dining hall was standing room only. All ninety-eight residents had shown up for Chef Pearl's taco surprise, a Manor favorite. And Irene Spencer's capture as the Walk'n Roll bandit added to the excitement. Lunch and a show.

The room buzzed with anticipation until Irene, leaning heavily on her old walker, creaked into the room.

Dead silence.

"What are you all gawking at? Don't get your Depends in a wad," blasted a red-faced Irene. "Eat your miserable lunches and mind your own business."

Irene creaked her way to the table where Edna and Beanie were finishing up their taco surprise.

"Irene!" Edna said with a smile. "How lovely you look

today."

"Bug off, Edna," Irene snarled. "You left a pile of glitter from that ridiculous cane right by my front door. I know you and your sidekick are up to your necks in this walker business."

"Sidekick?" Beanie protested. "I'm no sidekick. I'm as much the brains of this crime-fighting team as Edna. Now it's true she's the fashion plate, but I helped plan the heist. I'm the one who remembered the magnifying glass...."

Edna shook her head. "Beanie, hush."

"So, you admit it then?" Irene said with a self-satisfied smile. "I'll be speaking to Director Peabody-Jones about you two. You're out of here, once and for all."

"Can it, Irene. Old PBJ isn't going to do anything to us. You stole that walker from Florence, and everybody knows it." Edna was irate and determined.

Irene wasn't getting away with this.

"Whoa, get a load of that, will you?" Beanie's remark brought the argument to a standstill. She was staring in the direction of the dining room's main entrance.

Every bifocaled, cataract-laced eyeball turned to stare at the door. Dentures dropped. Forks clattered on china plates. "Wowzer," mumbled one old man, and several gray heads nodded in agreement.

At the doorway, the Manor's director, William Peabody-Jones — aka PBJ to the residents — stood with a full-figured woman dressed in a soft peach cashmere sweater and gray slacks. She was probably in her early sixties, but with the right makeup and lighting, could pass for at least a decade younger. Her shiny bottle-brunette hair, coiffed in a French twist, showed off her high cheekbones and huge brown eyes. Sort of like Audrey Hepburn, if she wore a size twelve.

PBJ's assistant, Kristina, rushed to the front of the dining room with her cellphone in hand. She took pictures of all the new residents and shared them online on the Magnolia Facebook page. She snapped one of Marjorie and PBJ and returned to her seat to finish her lunch.

"Look! She's not even wearing orthopedic shoes," Beanie remarked in admiration. "I haven't worn heels that high since the 1980s."

Stocky, squat PBJ was dressed in his usual rumpled blue suit and stained tie. His greasy comb-over was particularly shiny today. Must have treated himself to a brand-new tube of Brylcreem. Standing next to the stylish woman, the dowdy director looked like a frumpy Keebler elf.

PBJ pushed his spectacles higher on his nose and cleared his throat. "Ladies and gentlemen, it gives me great pleasure to introduce our newest resident. This is Marjorie Riley, and she has moved into one of our independent living cottages.

Let's give her a warm Magnolia Manor welcome."

A smattering of applause followed Marjorie and PBJ as they wove through the maze of tables. Irene angled her squeaky walker in their path, trying to get PBJ's attention.

"Director Peabody-Jones, I need to speak to you," she said.

"In just a minute, Mrs. Spencer. Let me get Mrs. Riley settled at her table." He gently nudged the walker out of his way. Irene turned on her heel and huffed and puffed her way out of the dining room.

The director watched her go, shaking his head in frustration. "She'll be fine," he mumbled to Marjorie. "Irene Spencer drums up more drama than the latest love triangle on 'Days of Our Lives.'"

Marjorie hid a smile behind her hand. She followed the

director to a table occupied by two ladies, both in their seventies. One had short-cropped salt and pepper hair, lovely brown eyes, and a bright, friendly smile. This must be Beanie, she decided. The other woman wore her shiny silver hair cut in a modern shoulder-length bob. Her makeup was flawless, her clothing stylish. Marjorie noticed Edna's assessing stare. This was a lady to be reckoned with.

"Marjorie, I'd like you to meet Edna Duncan and Bernice Buffala. You've been assigned to their table, and I know you'll all become great friends."

As he pulled out a chair for Marjorie, he whispered in her ear. "Just don't let them drag you into some of their ridiculous antics. These two have a way of finding trouble."

With a quick nod to the ladies, he hurried off to deal with Irene and her latest complaint.

"What a lovely sweater you're wearing, Marjorie. Isn't it beautiful, Edna?"

Beanie gushed.

Edna shifted uncomfortably in her chair. "If you don't mind wearing last year's style, I suppose it's fine," she sniffed.

"Don't mind her, Marjorie. Edna's used to being the best-dressed old woman in the room," Beanie said in a low voice. "It'll be nice to see her have a little competition."

Marjorie smiled at Edna. "As soon as I came in the room, I noticed your gorgeous blouse, Edna. That lavender is a perfect color for you. And such a flattering style."

Edna's face lit up. "Alfred Dunner's a fashion genius, isn't he?" All three ladies laughed. And a friendship was born.

*****

BACK IN HER COTTAGE after lunch, Marjorie unpacked unfamiliar keepsakes and arranged make-believe family pictures on the walls. Everything she touched was strange and new. Stephen and a couple of his assistants had selected the items for her. A souvenir mug from Niagara Falls from an imaginary honeymoon, a tacky statue of the Eiffel Tower bought on a make-believe twenty-fifth wedding anniversary trip. A framed lock of brown hair belonging to her imaginary son, Robert. Bronzed baby shoes from her "daughter" named Mabel. Mabel? Who named their daughter Mabel these days? She shook her head in despair.

This fabricated life was lonely and painful. But the alternative? Suppose they found her? Marjorie shuddered. Her life would be over, once and for all.

A knock on the cottage door made her jump. She rushed to the living room window and peered through the heavy drapes. A tall, trim man. Early sixties. A gray glen-plaid suit. Well-made but not too expensive. Wavy, brown hair. Broad shoulders. Hmmm. Who could this be?

Marjorie smoothed her hair and dress before unlocking the door. She flashed her best smile.

"Hello. May I help you?"

"Marjorie Riley? I'm Brett Hopewell, the new chaplain here at Magnolia. I missed you at lunch, so I wanted to stop by and introduce myself. I hope this isn't an inconvenient time." Pastor Hopewell flashed a charming smile as he gently shook her hand.

Hmmm. Something fishy about this one. He's trying just a little too hard.

She smiled back. "This is a perfect time. Please come in, Pastor. It's nice to meet you."

Marjorie waved at two nosy Nancys peering at her from across the street. The old women quickly turned back to their flower garden, but not before giving Marjorie the evil eye.

"Mind your own business," she mumbled under her breath and closed the door tightly.

"What a lovely family you have, Marjorie," Pastor Hopewell remarked as he scanned the photographs on the oak credenza. He picked up a framed picture of a family picnicking by a bubbling mountain brook. She had no idea who any of the people were. It had been placed on the table by whichever U.S. Marshal had furnished her house.

Pastor Hopewell peered at the photo. "Your daughter has your eyes, but your son must look like his father. And these grandchildren," he said. "Bet they keep you on your toes." He placed the picture back on the table.

Marjorie smiled faintly. "Oh, yes, they're quite a handful."

Anxious to change the subject, she asked, "So you mentioned you're the new chaplain here. Where are you from?"

"Oh, I'm an Atlanta boy, born right downtown in Grady hospital. Lived here all my life. How about you?"

Marjorie felt her palms moisten, her throat dry up. This was brand new territory for her, and she wasn't too sure she could lie her way through this conversation. "Keep it simple," Stephen had advised her during her orientation into the witness protection program.

So she did.

She remembered the back story that had been drilled into her. "I'm from Kansas," she said. And changed the subject again. "Would you care for some tea? I was just about to make a pot."

Not waiting for a response, Marjorie took off for the kitchen. Switching from Marjorie Sims to Marjorie Riley was going to be harder than she thought.

Four

Beanie's Discovery

"*Y*ou simply must do something about those two!" Irene spit out the words. Afraid her dentures might spring loose, Director Peabody-Jones slid down in his desk chair. When it came to irate residents, duck and cover was his motto.

"I made a simple mistake. Picked up the wrong walker. That's all." Irene pulled a wrinkled wad of tissues from her sweater sleeve and began dabbing at her moist forehead. The director noticed with concern that her hands were shaking. "But those women treated me like a criminal. In front of everyone in the dining room. It was humiliating."

"Now, Miss Irene, calm yourself. Beanie and Edna didn't mean any harm. They were just trying to help Florence get her walker back." He paused, gauging the level of Irene's anger. To his dismay, her face was getting redder by the minute. He could almost see her blood pressure shooting over the limit.

Her feathers were sorely ruffled this time.

"I'll have a talk with the ladies, Irene. They won't bother you anymore."

"See to it they don't, Director," Irene sniffed, her head high. "And remember, my son Theodore makes significant donations to this facility — with the understanding that I will live out my retirement years in a certain amount of comfort and ease. Do I need to talk to him about this situation?"

Now, the director knew Irene was slowly draining her son's bank account. He'd had numerous conversations with Theodore about his mother's insatiable appetite for catalog shopping. Her closet was packed full of slacks, sweaters, and shoes from dozens of catalogs that arrived weekly. Theodore had asked the director to dump all such incoming mail addressed to his mother into the office File 13. But it hadn't slowed Irene's shopping habit.

"Of course not, Miss Irene. There's no need to involve your son in this." The director rose from his chair and walked around to the front of his desk. He smiled at the old woman and patiently patted her arm. "Just let me take care of everything.

Now, why don't you go back to your room and have a nice nap?"

"I'm too keyed up to take a nap. Think I'll go for a walk. See if I can snatch a snack from the dining room." Her face was back to its normal hue, but there was no hiding the fury in her eyes. She turned at the office door to fire a parting shot.

"Just see to it that you handle those two pot stirrers."

"Yes, ma'am," he replied before firmly closing the door behind her. He could hear the rusty old walker squeak all the way down the hall. "No wonder she stole Florence's," he mumbled. "Hers IS a piece of junk."

*****

"So, TELL ME," Edna said as Beanie started up the golf cart. "How did you know PBJ kept the key under the mat? I thought he had it locked away in his office. Protected from people like you and me." Edna grinned. "He's gonna blow a fuse this time."

"It was a cinch. A couple of weeks ago, he was driving those bigwigs from the state government around the cottages. I just happened to be there when he got back, and I saw him hide the key." She smiled at Edna. "He's got to do better than that to hide something from us. Besides, we need this cart today. We haven't properly welcomed Marjorie, and these wheels make the perfect welcome wagon."

Beanie made a sharp left out of the Manor's parking lot and headed down toward the cottages. The Magnolia Manor complex was made up of two parts. The Manor itself, a warm, welcoming brick structure, contained three floors of comfortable apartments for residents who needed the extra care of assisted living. The other part was made up of a dozen well-kept cottages, painted in a variety of eye-pleasing pastels. The cottages provided homes for seniors who were happy living on their own. Golf cart paths wound around tall shade trees and immaculately kept gardens. It looked like the perfect place to enjoy the golden retirement years.

"Will you please slow down, Lead Foot? You're going to kill us both!" Edna gripped the edge of her seat with both hands. The white gift bag with blue ribbon containing Marjorie's 'welcome gift' was wedged between her feet. "Good thing Stephen's coming to help me with my exercises today. Your driving is killing my knee."

"I like that Stephen," Beanie remarked with a slightly wicked grin. "He's a real cutie. I'm thinking of getting my knee replaced just so he can come work on me." She waggled her eyebrows in a poor imitation of Groucho Marx. Edna couldn't help but laugh.

"Now, Beanie, Stephen's a looker, that's for sure. But he's too young for you. More Marjorie's speed. Besides, he's only here for a few weeks while Ronnie, my assigned physical therapist, is out of town taking care of his mother.

"And remember, this knee replacement hasn't exactly been a walk in the park, you know. Now slow down before you hurt us both."

"Oh, come on, Edna. This thing will only go 20 miles per hour." Beanie smiled. "Besides, I'm a great driver. Just ask the AARP. I aced their Defensive Driving for Seniors class. Got a framed certificate and everything."

Edna looked doubtful but decided to let that one pass. "There's 313, Marjorie's cottage." She pointed at the neat yellow building with cheery marigolds dotting the front flower bed. "But who's that?" A tall, slender man in a nice-looking suit was walking down the path from Marjorie's house.

"Oh, that's the new chaplain, Pastor Hopewell. You didn't come to the church service last Sunday, so you didn't hear about him. Quite a looker, isn't he? And he's single. A widower, I think. At least that's what the rumor mill says," replied Beanie, grinning. "He just got here last night. And here he is, already hard at work bringing comfort to the lonely and downtrodden, I'm sure."

She brought the golf cart to a full stop across the street from Marjorie's. The pastor gave them a friendly wave as he climbed into a sleek silver sedan and drove off.

"My, my," remarked Edna as she watched the car wind its way down the narrow street. "He should spark a little interest in the Wednesday evening Bible studies."

Both ladies laughed as they made their way to the front door. Edna's cane sprinkled glitter like fairy dust on the cracked sidewalk.

A slightly disheveled Marjorie greeted them at her door. "Edna and Beanie!

How nice that you came for a visit. Moving into a new home can be a little lonely." She smiled thinly as she ushered them into her living room. "Please excuse the mess. Still unpacking, you know."

Edna made herself comfortable on the plush sofa while Beanie perched on an elegant side chair. "Wow, nice digs, Marjorie," Beanie remarked as she rubbed her hand over the intricately carved arm of the well-made chair. "No Rooms to Go for you, huh?"

Marjorie wrung her hands nervously. "My late husband was a furniture maker," she replied. Her voice trembled slightly as she continued. "He insisted on only the best quality. He actually made that table." She gestured to the oak credenza that held all the phony family pictures.

Furniture maker? Why in the world did I say that? Marjorie shook her head in dismay. *I must be losing my mind.*

"Well, ummm," Marjorie stammered. "Would you ladies like some tea? I was just making some for Pastor Hopewell, but he was called away." She chewed on her lower lip.

Edna spoke up. "Marjorie, are you all right? You seem a little frazzled."

"Everything's fine, Edna. I guess I'm just a little overwhelmed. Moving and unpacking, so many new people."

"You sit right down, dear," said Beanie. "I'll get the tea, and then Edna and I will help you get things organized. Besides, you haven't even opened the gift we brought you."

Marjorie smiled and nodded. "Thanks, you two. Some hot tea and kind company is just what I need." She sat down at her dining room table and untied the ribbon on her present.

"Don't get too excited," Beanie quipped. "It's just a little something we give to all the new residents."

Inside the bag, Marjorie found a Magnolia Manor pen, a matching notepad, and a green and white "Start your day the Magnolia way" mug, packed full of chocolate kisses and peppermints. As she took the items out of the bag, the mug overturned, scattering kisses and peppermints across the floor.

"Don't worry. I've got them," said Beanie as she bent down to pick up the wayward candy. One of the kisses rolled under the credenza, and Beanie went down on all fours to retrieve it.

"Show off," Edna snickered, with just a little twinge of jealousy in her voice.

Beanie grabbed the candy, but not before she got a good look at the underside of Marjorie's table. She nearly banged her head when she tried to get back up.

"Beanie, are you all right?" Edna asked, clearly concerned about her friend.

"I'm fine," Beanie replied with a little laugh. "No worries." But from the look on her face, Edna knew something was up. Now wasn't the time, though. Beanie would share whatever she knew on the way back to the Manor, and Edna realized she'd just have to be patient.

After the ladies finished their tea, the trio got to work putting Marjorie's house in order. Within a couple of hours, closets were organized, knickknacks were unpacked, and the kitchen was neat as a pin.

But Edna was no closer to discovering Beanie's secret.

Curiosity was eating away at her.

Finally, Beanie stood with her hands on her hips and surveyed the tidy cottage. "I believe our work here is done," she said with a grin.

"Thank you so much for your help," said Marjorie. "It would have taken months for me to get this all done. You're angels, both of you."

That made Edna smile. "Angels? Uh, not exactly. Just ask Irene Spencer. We're just glad we could help. But I'm exhausted." She glanced at her watch. "And we even have enough time for a nap before dinner. Will we see you in the dining room tonight?"

Beanie piped up. "You need to come early. It's salmon patties tonight, Chef Pearl's specialty."

"As lovely as that sounds, I think I'll just cozy up to the Hallmark channel with a nice bowl of soup. I'm worn out, too."

Marjorie walked the women to her door. "Thanks again for your help. I'll see you in the morning."

Beanie and Edna waved as they sped off in the golf cart. Once they were out of sight of the cottage, Edna demanded to know what Beanie had discovered.

Beanie pulled the cart to the curb and turned to her friend. "Marjorie said her husband had made that beautiful credenza in her living room, right?"

"Yes. So?" Edna's patience was wearing thin.

"So why did it have a stamp on the underside that says 'Ashley Home Furnishings'? I think our new friend is up to something."

Five

Pearl Porter

*P*earl let the screen door slam shut behind her. "Mama?" she called as she struggled with the plastic grocery bags tangled around her wrists. The living room was sweltering and smelled of tuna fish and stale coffee. Mama's lunch.

Pearl heard the TV blaring in the bedroom. As usual, Dr. Phil was dispensing his pop psychology advice to another desperate family. Mama never missed his show.

Pearl sighed. *He's really wound up today. And he'll have Mama all riled up about the crazy folks on TV who can't take care of their own problems. That's all she'll want to talk about at supper.*

"Mama? I'm home!" she called out again, peeling the bags off her sticky arm and dropping them onto the worn kitchen table. Once she finished preparing the evening meal at the Manor, she was free to go home to care for her mother. The kitchen crew took care of the dinner clean-up and the breakfast prep.

Today on the way home, she'd stopped at Kroger to pick up some bare essentials. She pulled the items out of the bags and put them away. Eggs, milk, orange juice, coffee, bread. Mama's favorite pecan shortbread cookies. The usual.

And then there was Mama's new pill. The miracle medicine that doctors thought might keep her heart disease at bay — a drug called Cholestopine — went in the kitchen cabinet along with the rest of her prescriptions. High blood pressure, high cholesterol, diabetes, thyroid pills.

Pearl sighed. How much more would her mother have to endure?

"Hey, Baby," Mama replied, raising her voice to be heard over the TV's din.

"Could you bring me a cool drink? It's hot as Hades back here."

"Yes, ma'am."

She poured Mama a glass of iced tea, added a pink packet of sweetener, and made her way to the back bedroom. The old wood floors creaked as she walked down the hall, pausing as she always did to run her fingers over the black and white photo of Daniel, the love of her life. Gone nearly twenty years now.

Snatched away by a heart attack on a hot August night.

"Hey, my love." Her finger paused a moment on his yellowed cheek.

It was just her and Mama living together in this big house Daddy had bought when Pearl was a little girl. She and her big brother, John, had grown up together here running up and down this very hall, chasing and yelling, laughing and teasing. Pearl smiled at the memories. But then John turned eighteen and enlisted, becoming a proud Marine. He left for Afghanistan a decade ago and never came back.

Daddy's heart shattered into a million pieces when he got the news about John. He didn't live long after that.

Now a picture of John in his uniform, all toothy grin and youthful over-confidence, hung on one side of Daniel. Daddy, standing tall and strong on the front porch of this very house, hung on the other side.

The three men of Pearl's life. They were supposed to be there to help her, protect her, keep her safe from the dangers of this world. But they were gone. She was alone. And now, all the responsibility of caring for Mama fell to her.

Pearl tapped lightly on her mother's door to let her know she was there. Mama was startled easily these days. Jumping and grabbing her heart at the slightest noise. Pearl didn't want to frighten her.

She found her Mama sitting comfortably in her ancient rocking chair. She'd rocked both her babies in that chair, and the teeth marks — hers and John's — were still visible as tiny scratches in the dark wood stain. Her simple aluminum walker stood next to the chair, ready to help Mama get to her bed or the bathroom.

"Well, don't you look pretty," Pearl said, smiling. Mama did look nice. Her silver hair was neatly combed, her house dress clean and pressed. She wore comfortable, sturdy sandals. Pearl thought she even spied a touch of lipstick and a little blush on her crinkled cheeks.

"Caroline insisted," Mama said. "She makes me take a bath, washes my hair. Even put on this ridiculous makeup." Mama's hand shook as she touched her cheek to brush off the offending powder.

Even though she complained, Pearl knew Mama was proud

of the way she looked. Didn't matter that her mother was ninety-one. Ladies, especially southern ones, liked to look pretty.

And Pearl knew she was blessed to still have Mama with her. She really didn't mind the extra trips to the store, the doctor appointments, the same TV shows every night. Pearl loved listening to Mama's stories, especially the ones about her and John.

"What did you have for lunch today?" Pearl asked. She knew it had been the usual tuna fish sandwich on wheat bread, but she wanted to see if Mama could remember. On some days, the good ones, she had no problem remembering, and she was more like her old self, the fifth-grade school teacher who calculated fractions in a split second and worked long division problems in her head. But on other days, the not-so-good ones, she couldn't even recall what year it was.

Today was a not-so-good one.

"Oh, I don't know," Mama said impatiently. She waved her hand dismissively. "Don't ask me such hard questions."

"OK, Mama," Pearl replied, patting her mother's hand. "You just finish watching your TV show while I fix dinner. You hungry?"

"I would like some fried chicken, cole slaw, and homemade biscuits," she told Pearl, her tone imperious. "And be sure you don't burn the biscuits. You know how you always do."

Pearl shook her head as she walked to the kitchen. Once, when she was thirteen, she'd let the biscuits stay in the oven too long, and Mama'd never let her forget it. Now her mother couldn't remember what she'd had for lunch, but those burned biscuits from forty years ago were seared into her memory.

When Pearl opened the oven, she was delighted to find a pan of fried chicken, hot and ready to be served. Coleslaw was chilling on the bottom shelf of the refrigerator, and a basket of biscuits had been tucked into the microwave to stay warm.

Caroline, you are a godsend.

Pearl smiled. Dinner was ready, so she could take a quick break before she fed Mama. The mail was piled neatly on the table, another telltale sign that Caroline had been here, and Pearl pulled out a chair to have a look at the assortment of letters, bills, and junk mail. One envelope from Mama's Medicare program caught her eye. She slit it open; her heart filled with dread.

This can't be good. No good news ever seems to come from the insurance company.

As usual, this letter was filled with medical and legal jargon, impossible for the average folk to understand. But what Pearl could decipher was not good news.

Apparently, Mama's coverage was changing, and her insurance would no longer cover her heart medicine, Cholestopine.

And from what I remember when I looked it up on the internet, Cholestopine costs almost $800 each month. How in the world are we going to pay that?

Pearl quickly crunched the numbers in her head. She made a good living at Magnolia Manor. And Mama's social security check helped keep their heads above water. But this house needed so much work. A new heating and air conditioning system. A new roof to fend off the autumn rains. And the plumbing was plum worn out. There was just no way these ends were going to meet.

But Mama had to have that medicine.

Daniel. Daddy. John. My three angels. You're all going to have to pitch in and help me with this. I can't do it alone.

Six

A Death at the Manor

"*P*earl outdid herself this time," Beanie said through a mouthful of salmon. "Best patties ever."

Edna agreed. "She does have a way with canned fish products, that's for sure. Too bad Marjorie missed this." Edna motioned to the untouched food cooling at Marjorie's place.

"She must have forgotten to call the kitchen to let them know she wouldn't be coming to dinner," said Beanie. "And you know how upset Pearl gets about that. Hope she doesn't come down too hard on her. Rookie mistake."

"Well, Pastor Hopewell is certainly no rookie." Edna pointed her fork at the new pastor who was making conversation with some residents on the other side of the dining hall. "He was helping Pearl and her staff serve dinner when I came in. In fact, he actually brought our food to the table and introduced himself to me. Nice man," Edna sighed. "Reminds me a little of my late husband, James. Tall, dark, handsome. Smile like sunshine."

"Pastor Hopewell sure knows how to work a room," said Beanie, her mouth full of salmon. "Look at Irene staring up at him with those big cow eyes. As if she'd have a chance with him." She looked over at her friend. "But if you were just a decade younger, you'd catch his eye for sure." She gave Edna's hand a squeeze.

Edna squeezed back. "You bet I would." They both laughed.

"Besides," Beanie was quick to point out, "Just look at the way Charlie Richardson keeps eyeing you. He remembers you from high school, right?" She pointed her fork in the old man's direction. His face lit up when he saw Edna looking at him.

Edna's heart melted each time she saw Charlie. She remembered how he was then. So young and vibrant and strong. "He's an old, dear friend, Beanie. We actually went to the Jonesboro High School prom together many, many years ago. He was quite a handsome young man back then."

"What happened to you two?" Beanie spewed hush puppy crumbs as she spoke.

Edna smiled. "He ditched me at the senior class picnic. We were entered into a canoe race, and he never showed up. I suspected he was out in the woods with pretty Reba Moulder. We had one huge fight, and that was that.

"We tried to remain friends, but you know how kids are. After graduation, he went to Georgia Tech, and I went to Berry College. We just grew apart. Then he met Lisa, and I met James, and we didn't see each other very much after that.

"I do remember how brilliant he was, though. Excellent mathematician. Worked for NASA for a while, but he left there and ended up doing some other kind of government work. Not sure what. I was sorry to hear about Lisa's death last year. And now he's facing Alzheimer's disease all alone. No children or other family to help."

Beanie gave her a sympathetic smile. "He's got us, Edna. Interesting that he remembers you. You haven't seen each other for forty years?"

"A nurse explained that to me. She said your memory is like an inexpensive bookshelf you might get at Walmart. The books on the bottom shelf are tucked in tight and don't move, even when the bookshelf is shaken. But the books on the higher shelves aren't as secure and can fall down or tumble out of place if the bookshelf is rocked.

"That's a lot like memory loss. Charlie can remember things that happened four decades ago, but he hasn't got a clue how to make a cup of coffee."

"Well, you and I will do everything we can to help him," said Beanie. "And he sure does have a charming smile." The two ladies watched as Charlie's nurse helped him out of the dining room. He gave Edna a little wave as he left.

Beanie saw Hurricane Irene roaring toward them before Edna did.

"Oh, great," moaned Beanie. "What do you suppose she wants?"

"Let's not be rude, Beanie. Just put your head down and pretend you're still eating. Maybe she'll go away." Edna stuffed a roll in her mouth.

Irene's walker ka-thumped, ka-thumped its way to their table. "Where's your new friend?" she asked, her eyes glued to Marjorie's plate. "Not coming to dinner tonight? Is she feeling poorly?"

"No, just tired from unpacking boxes all day," Beanie answered, her mouth packed with coleslaw. "Nice of you to be concerned, though." She stared down at her plate, wishing with all her heart that Irene would go away.

"Well, it would be a sin to let this food go to waste, wouldn't it?" Irene offered up a simpering smile. "Do you suppose she'd mind if I just took a little bit back to Mr. Whiskers? He loves Pearl's salmon patties."

Without waiting for an answer, Irene scooped up Marjorie's salmon with a napkin and tucked it into her pocket. Pointing her walker toward the door, she made a beeline for the hallway. *Ka-thump, ka-thump, ka-thump. Squeak, squeak.*

And she was gone.

Edna shook her head. "That Irene's a piece of work, that's for sure." But thinking better of her unkind words, she added a truly Southern "Bless her heart."

Beanie mumbled, "I think you have to make sure she has one before you can bless it."

"Beanie!" Edna scolded. "That was awful. She needs our prayers more than our snarky comments."

"You're right. I'm sorry." Beanie looked repentant, but Edna had her doubts.

"You know, she's probably just lonely," Edna said. "No one comes to visit her except her son, and he only comes when the bill is due. He never takes her anywhere or spends any real time with her. Imagine what that would be like?"

"You're right," Beanie said, and she really was repentant this time. "I need to learn to be nicer to her. She just makes it so darn difficult."

Edna eyed her friend intently. "Apparently, we need a little extra spiritual teaching tonight. If you know what I mean."

"OK, OK, Edna, stop with the glaring. Let's go. Especially since there's no ice cream for dessert. Did you hear the delivery truck got stuck under the railroad bridge? Again! I know it's the fastest route to the interstate highway, but wouldn't you think the driver would have learned that his truck just can't fit under that bridge?" Beanie shook her head. "And I was really looking forward to some mint chocolate chip."

Edna smiled. "Me, too. Guess that underpass is the Lord's way of keeping us slim and trim." Edna sipped her tea thoughtfully. "If a trucker doesn't know what he's doing, he can get his truck stuck in there like a cork in a bottle. Last time, the driver had to let some air out of his tires so the truck could get through."

"I remember." Beanie shook her head sadly. "All the ice cream melted. Such a tragedy."

When she finished her tea, Edna grabbed her cane and slowly raised herself from the table. She let out a little groan when she took her first step.

"What's wrong, Edna?" Beanie asked, alarmed. "I thought you had physical therapy today. Did Stephen cancel on you?"

"No, he came, but I'm just a little sore. His magic fingers were rougher than I'm used to. I think he's a rookie. Good thing he's cute, or I'd be tempted to hurt him." She straightened her back as she headed for the door. "I'll be fine tomorrow.

After all, no pain, no gain."

"Maybe so, but this seems like more hurt than what it's worth." She held on to Edna's arm and guided her to the door. "C'mon. We're still in time for front-row seats. And I want a bird's eye view of this new pastor."

They settled into their seats and watched as the other residents, mostly old women, filed through the doors. No Baptist woman worth her salt would miss a Wednesday evening Bible study, come locusts, frogs, or hail like fire.

"Good evening, everyone." Pastor Hopewell was seated at the piano. His voice was smooth as Kentucky whiskey and just as intoxicating. The ladies were mesmerized.

"Let's begin with an oldie but goodie," the pastor said with a bright smile. "Everyone turn to page 312 in your hymnal. I'll Fly Away. Let's lift our voices and sing praises to the Lord this evening!"

Pastor Hopewell's fingers danced across the keyboard in a raucous rendition of the old hymn that had every arthritic knee in the joint jumping.

"Wow," was all Beanie could say. Edna nodded in agreement, her face flushed.

"Now, let's get down to studying God's Word. I thought I'd start with an old favorite. John 3:16. Will you recite it with me?"

"For God so loved the world," the enthusiastic crowd recited in chorus.

Pastor Hopewell beamed down on his congregation. "Ah, a choir of angels could not have sounded more beautiful. Now, let's talk about what these words mean to each of us today."

He taught for over an hour, but no one minded. In fact, no one moved, except for the occasional head nod or "Amen!" When the lesson was finally over, Pastor Hopewell tucked his shiny leather Bible under his arm and shook each hand as his happy congregation filed out through the wide chapel doors.

When it was Edna's turn, she waved Beanie to go on without her. Then she took the pastor's hand and pulled him into the hall.

"Why, Miss Edna, is everything OK?" Pastor Hopewell said. "Where's your friend, Miss Marjorie? I noticed she wasn't at dinner tonight."

"Oh, she's just a little worn out from all the excitement of moving. She decided she'd stay home and rest this evening," Edna explained. "But Pastor, I have a small prayer request. My knee is hurting me something awful, and I'd feel so much better if I knew you were praying for me."

"Oh, Miss Edna, I'll be happy to pray for you. But don't forget to do what the doctor tells you. Remember, the Bible says, "The Good Lord helps those who help themselves." And then he flashed that dazzling smile, turned, and headed toward his office.

Edna stood in the middle of the hallway, flabbergasted. *No, that's not at all what the Bible says. Every good Baptist preacher learns that on his first day in seminary. Something's not right about our Pastor Hopewell. And I'm just the one to figure it out.*

"Help! Help! Something's wrong with Mr. Whiskers!"

Edna turned when she heard Irene scream. She rushed down the hall to Irene's room, and there she saw Beanie holding Mr. Whiskers. The cat was not moving, and Beanie shook her head at Edna.

"Irene, let's take Mr. Whiskers to the staff room. Maybe one of the nurses can help us," said Edna. Irene nodded, and Beanie led the way with Mr. Whiskers as still as stone in her arms.

Edna knocked on the staff room door. Stephen appeared, a cup of coffee in his hands. He studied the sad little group before he carefully took the cat from Beanie. "What happened, Miss Irene?" he asked softly. He examined the cat gently while Irene told him about Mr. Whiskers' symptoms.

"Well, first, he seemed a little agitated. Kept pacing up and down the room. Didn't want me to touch him. He began to drool, and then he threw up. That's when I picked him up and put him on his cushion. He just lay there, so still. Didn't move a muscle." Irene wrung her hands. Tears filled her eyes. "What's wrong with my sweet kitty?"

"Can you tell me what he's had to eat tonight?" Stephen gently massaged the cat's abdomen. His expression was serious.

"Well, let's see. His usual cat chow, a piece of an oatmeal cookie, a strawberry — he loves strawberries, you see — and a spoonful of vanilla ice cream."

Beanie and Edna exchanged looks. Edna rolled her eyes. *What a nutcase.*

Irene paused, thinking. "Oh, and some of the salmon patty I brought back from the dining room. Is he going to be alright?"

Stephen shook his head sadly. "I'm sorry, Miss Irene, but I'm afraid there's nothing we can do. Mr. Whiskers has passed away. I think he may have been poisoned."

MAGNOLIA
MANOR

Seven

The Flooding of the Chattahoochee

$\mathcal{M}$arjorie hit the power button on the remote and turned off the TV. She'd watched two sappy Hallmark movies back to back, from cheery start to tear-jerking finale. She'd sworn off the network's soapy mysteries after that terrible night in the parking garage. Then she'd gotten hooked on the romance movies.

But tonight had just about cured her. She'd had all she could take of the cookie-cutter flicks — pretty young women leaving their promising, satisfying careers to run off with a handsome but shallow man in order to live happily ever after.

Silly. Just plain silly. Oh, well. There's always the Christmas marathon.

Nonstop jingle bells from October through January.

Marjorie was startled by a knock on the door. She looked through the tiny peephole and yanked the heavy door open to let the white-clad visitor into the room and out of the harsh porch light.

"What are you doing here?" she asked, dragging him into the living room. "I thought we were only to have contact if there was an emergency." She saw something in his eyes that hadn't been there before: fear.

"Oh, so there is an emergency," she said. "What's going on?"

"I think you're in danger," Stephen said. "Irene Spencer's cat died tonight.

Pretty sure it was poisoned."

"A cat died? And I'm in danger?" Marjorie shook her head. "A little far-fetched, don't you think?"

"We think the food that contained the poison was taken from your plate. The salmon you were supposed to be eating with Beanie and Edna tonight. But you didn't show, so Irene bagged it up for the cat. A couple of hours later, we've got one dead Mr. Whiskers on our hands. The crime lab is investigating to see what kind of poison was used," said Stephen. "But I think you're the target, Marjorie. Somehow, Kingpin must have found you."

Marjorie slumped down onto the couch. "What am I going to do?" she asked Stephen, her panic rising. "Should I leave?"

"My boss will need a couple of days to set up a new identity for you. A new place to live, new cover. Until then, I'm moving you into the Manor. There's an empty room near Edna and Beanie that's used as a guest room. It should be safe enough for now. And I'll be there to keep an eye on things."

Marjorie asked, "Edna and Beanie were just here today, helping me unpack. They're pretty sharp cookies. How am I going to explain my sudden move to the Manor?"

"I'm afraid your pipes sprung a leak." Stephen grinned, looking around the room. "Just throw some clothes in a suitcase, and I'll take you in my car. I'll fix the pipes so it'll look like the Chattahoochee River came barreling through here in flood stage. That'll convince everyone. Can't have our newest resident living with soaked carpet and wet walls, can we?"

Within an hour, Marjorie was hanging clothes in her new closet, in a safe room tucked between Beanie's and Edna's. She liked having her new buddies close, although she knew they wouldn't be much help in a real emergency. Edna could probably knock a bad guy over the head with her cane, maybe blind him with glitter. And Beanie could summon help on her "I've-fallen-and-I-can't-get-up" alert button.

Not much protection against Kingpin and his minions.

But still, she felt a little safer knowing they were nearby. Through one wall, she could hear Edna laughing at something the Beaver said to big brother Wally.

Through the other, she heard Beanie's raucous snoring. The noise was comforting. And besides, she kept telling herself, Stephen was just down the hall.

So, she crawled into bed, pulled the covers up over her head, and fell into a fitful sleep. Her dreams were packed full of screeching cats and dangerous strangers lurking in dark elevator corners. She even thought she smelled poison-tinged salmon patties frying. It was not a restful night.

She showered and dressed the next morning, well before the sun came up. She needed to choose her clothes carefully. She wanted to look as normal as possible to protect her cover, and part of that was dressing like 'Marjorie Riley' would dress on any given day. Truth be told, she'd prefer to spend the day in a sweatshirt and old jeans, cowering under her bed. But she refused to live the rest of her life afraid of her own shadow.

And soon as she could get online, she was going to restock her MaceFace pepper spray.

So, Marjorie decided a bright floral tunic with tan linen pants would fit the bill for a retired Topeka teacher. A pearl pendant with matching earrings completed the outfit. But if anyone looked at her closely — as she was sure Edna would — the dark circles under her eyes would be a tipoff that all was not well. She did her best with a cover stick and some blush, then pulled her hair back in a ponytail. She sighed at her reflection in the mirror. Not great, but it would have to do.

And why do I even bother? If Kingpin gets to me, he certainly won't care if I'm wearing flats or heels when he puts a gun to my head. Marjorie shivered at the thought.

A light knock on the door was all it took to make her jump out of her skin, but she relaxed a little when she saw Stephen peering back at her through the peephole. He looked worried.

"There's good news and bad news," he said as he came through the door. "First, the bad news. It's going to take them longer than they thought to get a new identity in place for you. So, you're going to have to stay put."

"And the good news?" Marjorie asked solemnly.

"We have a lead on Kingpin's location. A task force is tracking him right now. This may be over sooner than you think. And in the meantime, help is on the way. Several more agents have been assigned to your case." Stephen rested his hand lightly on her shoulder. "It's going to be fine. I'm not going to let anything happen to you, OK?"

Marjorie nodded, tears filling her large, dark eyes. "Thank you," she whispered. She hugged him tightly.

"Knock, knock!" Not waiting for a reply, Beanie and Edna

burst into the room. Stephen and Marjorie jumped apart, but not before the two old ladies got an eyeful.

"Oh, my. So sorry to interrupt," Edna said with a sly smile. She looked fresh as a daisy in her yellow blouse and white slacks. Her makeup was flattering, and her hair was carefully styled. In spite of herself, Marjorie smiled. *Bet she was a stunner a couple decades ago.*

Edna spoke first. "Beanie and I both heard noise coming through the walls of this room, and we figured we had a new neighbor." She lifted the familiar white gift bag tied with blue ribbon. "We even brought a welcome present. Looks like you're getting your own special welcome, though, huh?" Edna raised her eyebrows in a way that made Stephen laugh.

Then it was Beanie's turn. "Marjorie, what are you doing here? Did you change your mind about living in the cottage? It looked so homey after we'd put away all your things. I mean, these rooms are perfectly nice, and we'd love having you as a neighbor, but all your beautiful furniture would never fit in here."

Beanie looked from Marjorie to Stephen and back again, waiting for an explanation. Dressed in pink plaid capris and a faded blue tee-shirt that read "World's Greatest Nana," Beanie was the anti-Edna. Her spiky hair begged for a curling iron, and she hadn't bothered with makeup. Still, her warm smile lit up the room.

"Miss Beanie, Miss Edna," Stephen began, "Marjorie's cottage flooded last night. A broken pipe. Such a mess. Carpet and walls soaked. I happened to be in the office when she called for help. We packed up a few of her things and moved her in here around midnight. Sorry if we disturbed you. I just came by to check on her this morning."

"Oh, Marjorie! That's terrible!" Beanie put her arms around her friend and Edna patted her arm.

"We'll all go over to the cottage later and help you get everything you need," said Edna. "And while you're our next-door neighbor, just think of all the trouble we can get into." She winked at her friend.

Marjorie and Stephen exchanged looks, but Edna pretended not to notice. She just eyed them suspiciously.

I wonder what THAT'S all about!

Eight

Edna Cracks the Code

"*C*'mon, everybody. Time for breakfast." Beanie tugged on Marjorie's sleeve. "Everything will seem much better after we get a little hot coffee in you."

But chaos, not coffee, greeted them just outside the dining room. Crime scene tape blocked off the kitchen. A half-dozen plain clothes policemen were conducting a thorough search of the room while uniformed officers guarded the entrances. Pearl sat at a table in the back of the room with a detective, answering questions. She looked worried.

Meanwhile, wheelchairs and walkers formed a geriatric traffic jam in the hallway.

"Whoa, check out all the cops!" Beanie said, peering through the crowd.

"What's going on?" Edna asked Director Peabody-Jones above the noisy residents. The crowd of impatient seniors was turning into a hangry mob.

"The report came back on Miss Irene's cat. It really was poisoned, and the police suspect it might have something to do with yesterday's salmon patties. The kitchen's closed until they finish up their investigation," replied the director.

"Excuse me while I try to calm everyone down."

PBJ gently pushed his way to the front of the noisy throng.

"I need your attention, please," he said meekly. When everyone continued talking, PBJ pushed his glasses up on his nose, hiked up his pants, and bellowed, "If you want your breakfast, you need to be quiet and listen to me!"

Mouths slammed shut as every eye turned to the director.

"That's better," he said in his normal meek and mild voice, but his face had turned red from the strain. "First Baptist Church down the road has heard about our plight, and their Fellowship Sunday School class has volunteered to serve us some breakfast. And since it's such a beautiful morning, we've decided to dine al fresco. That means we're eating outside, for all you good ole boys." He offered up a weak smile.

"If you'll all move to the patio, the folks have already started setting up a delicious buffet."

A stampede of orthopedic shoes took off for the patio. Marjorie and Edna jumped out of the way, but Beanie fought her way to the front of the line. "I bet these church ladies can cook!" she hollered over her shoulder. "I'll save you some grits if I can, but you better get a move on."

By the time Marjorie and Edna got to the patio, Beanie was comfortably seated at a wrought iron table, a plate full of food in front of her. She'd managed to save two chairs for her friends.

"You've got to try these grits," said Beanie. "As my late husband Stan would say, they're DEE-licious!" She jammed a spoonful into her mouth and rolled her eyes in delight.

Edna smiled at Marjorie, and they made their way to the buffet line. The Baptist ladies, decked out in red and white striped aprons, handed them heaping plates of fluffy scrambled eggs and light-as-air biscuits. Marjorie's stomach turned in protest, but she smiled at the ladies as she took her plate. No need to hurt their feelings. And besides, she had to eat to keep her strength up. She poured herself a cup of coffee and joined her friends at the table.

The sunny Georgia weather, a big change from the piles of dirty snow and bitterly cold winds still pounding Philly this time of year, lifted her spirits. She sat back in her chair and sipped her coffee, all the while listening to her new friends bicker about the best way to make grits. Marjorie didn't care. The food was delicious.

To die for, as the kids would say? Well, let's hope not.

Just then, a shadow fell over the table. Irene Spencer stood between Beanie and Edna, blocking the sun. "So, Edna," she asked, "are you and Beanie going to sign up for Pastor Hopewell's talent showcase? Maybe teach your ridiculous dance group a new routine? Heaven knows, you could use a new one."

"What are you talking about, Irene? What talent showcase?" Edna didn't have a clue.

Irene let out a haughty little laugh. "Oh, so you don't know? My, my. I thought you knew everything about everything that went on here. Looks like you've missed something."

"Spill it, Irene." Edna was not in the mood for Irene's snippy comments.

"Well, everyone was so distressed about Mr. Whiskers' death and the police investigation and all, Pastor Hopewell thought it'd be a good idea to put on a little talent show this weekend to cheer us up. I'll be singing, of course."

Beanie made a face behind Irene's back. Marjorie covered her smile with her hand.

Irene continued. "You better hurry if you want to be in the show. The signup sheet is in the main office, and it's almost full. Be a shame if you missed the chance to share the stage with me." Irene turned toward the patio doors, singing an off-key version of "Do Re Mi" at the top of her lungs.

"She certainly is in good spirits for someone whose beloved cat just died," Edna said, puzzled by Irene's nonchalant attitude. She shrugged her shoulders and turned to Beanie. "Why don't you dash over to the office and see if you can get us signed up for the show. Can't let Irene have all the fun."

"On it, Edna." Beanie took off like a shot. A silver-haired, seventy-year-old bullet. She'd had lots of coffee this morning, and it showed.

Marjorie smiled. "You and Beanie sing?" she asked.

"Oh, no. Neither one of us can carry a tune in a bucket." She winked slyly. "But we're A-number-one dancers. We have a little troupe made up of a half dozen of the best old-lady dancers you've ever seen. We bring down the house with our rendition of John Anderson's 'Swingin'.'"

Marjorie eyed Edna's cane hanging on the back of her chair. "That doesn't slow you down?"

"Heavens, no!" Edna replied. "In fact, it's part of the act. Everybody in the troupe uses one, whether they need it or not. That's why we call ourselves the Raisin' Canes.

Marjorie smiled. "Cute."

"Think that's funny? The Presbyterians over at the Sunset Home call their dance group the Johnny Walkers. They all use red Walk'n Rolls in their routines." Edna leaned in close and lowered her voice to a whisper. "Their after-performance parties are notorious."

Marjorie laughed out loud for the first time in weeks. It felt good.

Edna studied Marjorie. "Would you like to join us? We could use some fresh blood in the act. And I can't dance with this bum knee. You could take my place. How about it?"

Marjorie shook her head. "No way. If you'd ever seen me dance, you'd take back that offer quick as a wink."

"Don't worry about a thing. We'll teach you. It'll be fun." Edna was not going to take 'no' for an answer.

By the time Stephen walked up with his plate, the other residents had returned to their rooms or gone off to scheduled activities like Brett Hopewell's morning devotion, a real crowd-pleaser. So PBJ was the only other diner. He sat alone at a small table on the other side of the patio, thoroughly enjoying another portion of bacon and eggs. There were already two dirty plates stacked in the corner of his table.

When Beanie came back from the office, she flashed Edna a grin and a thumbs-up sign. She sat down, and the women slid their chairs to make room for Stephen at the small table. Beanie didn't even give the young man a chance to swallow a bite of bacon before she started with her questions.

"So, what's going on now?" she asked, sipping a fresh cup of coffee. "Have you talked to any of the police? Is Pearl all right? Have they arrested anyone?" Beanie's eyes were too glittery and bright to be normal, and her left leg was performing a Riverdance jig under the table.

"Sorry, Stephen," Edna patted Stephen's arm. "That's Beanie's fourth cup of coffee. And as you can probably tell, she's not a fan of decaf."

"I really don't know any more than you do, Miss Beanie." Stephen gave her a patient smile. "It looks to me like the investigators are wrapping things up, and we should be able to have lunch in the dining room as usual." He dug his fork into the pile of eggs on his plate.

Just then, Director Peabody-Jones passed their table, a stack of dirty plates in one hand and his cellphone in the other. "Stephen's correct, ladies. The police are still questioning Pearl, but they should be leaving as soon as they finish with her. I just got a text from the man in charge."

"You ladies enjoy your morning," he continued, nodding his head politely. He trudged across the patio and dropped the plates in a bin of soapy water next to the buffet table.

But before he left the patio, the director turned and shot Stephen a pointed look. Stephen nodded slightly, a response that caught Edna's eye.

"OK, that's it," she blurted out. "All these secret stares and covert glances. There's something up with you and Marjorie, Stephen. And now I can see that PBJ is in on it, too. You may as well spill it, because Beanie and I will figure it out one way or another."

Marjorie looked horrified. Stephen's jaw fell open. Even Beanie stared at her friend in shock. "Edna, what are you talking about?" she asked.

"Well, let's start at the beginning," said Edna. "Marjorie, we know your husband was not a furniture maker. Beanie saw the Ashley furniture stamp on the bottom of your credenza. That's the first strange thing we noticed. Why would you lie about something like that, Marjorie?" She put up her index finger, signaling number one.

"Furniture maker?" Incredulous, Stephen whispered to Marjorie. "Where did that come from?"

Marjorie shook her head and shrugged her shoulders.

Edna continued. "Next, Irene's cat gets itself poisoned, probably by something in our dining room, and the police are called to investigate. Turns out the poison could be from the salmon patty on Marjorie's plate since nobody else who ate salmon got sick. Did you honestly think I didn't pick up on that?" She held up two fingers. "That's number two.

"Here's number three. How do you explain the fact that you always seem to be hanging around Marjorie, Stephen? Like in her room this morning. What were you really doing there? Doesn't add up." Edna crossed her arms and sat back in her chair, looking from Marjorie to Stephen and back again.

Stephen let out a deep sigh. "OK, Edna. You've got us. But we can't talk here. Meet us at Marjorie's cottage in half an hour, and I'll explain everything. If anyone asks where you're going, tell them you're helping Marjorie move her things up to the Manor because of the water damage. That should satisfy even the nosiest folks."

Stephen looked at Marjorie. "Go to your room and wait there. Don't go anywhere without me. Understood?"

Marjorie nodded. "I'll be sure to listen for the secret knock," she said with a small smile.

Edna cut in. "Secret knock? What are you two up to?" She shook her head. "OK, we'll head down to the cottage and start packing up her things, but you better be ready to tell us what's going on. If something's up with our friend Marjorie, we want to help."

Nine

Time to Fess Up, Marjorie

"*Y*ou wanted to see me, William?" Stephen asked as he tapped on the open office door. PBJ nodded, and Stephen closed the door. They shook hands warmly.

"Good to see you, Stephen. Have a seat. Seems like we haven't had a chance to catch up since you got here." PBJ pointed to the chair in front of his desk. "Is the Marshals Service everything Dad promised it would be?" William Peabody-Jones and Stephen Breckinridge had been friends since college. It was actually the director's dad, a Marshal himself, who had steered Stephen toward his career.

Stephen chuckled. "Well, it's an adventure, that's for sure. Never thought my PT training would come in handy, but so far, everyone seems to believe I'm Ronnie's replacement."

William nodded. "The residents seem to like you well enough, so your cover's secure. But we need to figure out this

Marjorie Riley situation. Tell me what you know so far."

"Well, sir, we know Irene's cat was poisoned, and the lab found strychnine in its system. Probably from the salmon patty on Marjorie's plate."

"Strychnine!" PBJ was flabbergasted. "There was strychnine in Pearl's salmon patties? Could it have come from somewhere in the Manor?"

"We're not sure yet," Stephen said. "It's a common ingredient in certain kinds of rat poison. The maintenance crew could have some in the utility building. But I'm sure it's easy enough to order online."

PBJ nodded. "Let's check that out. See if you can find the source of the poison. Now, is there any word from my former colleagues at the FBI about Kingpin?" the director asked. The director had disappointed his father and chosen to join the FBI instead of following in his dad's footsteps. It had been a point of friendly contention in his family for years. The staff at the Manor had no idea their beloved director was a highly decorated FBI agent. PBJ liked it better that way. "They suspect he's hiding out somewhere in the Atlanta area, just as you thought, William. It's an all-hands-on-deck situation for Georgia law enforcement.

He'll make a misstep soon enough, and we'll catch him when he does."

PBJ looked thoughtful. "How's Marjorie holding up?"

"So far, so good," Stephen answered. "She got a little shook last night when we had to move her into the Manor, but for the most part, she's been a real trooper. Even caught her singing songs about Kansas. Something about being corny in autumn."

PBJ laughed. "*South Pacific*. One of my favorites."

"Marjorie feels it's her duty to introduce me to every musical ever written."

Stephen shook his head. "But at least she's in pretty good spirits."

"Do Beanie and Edna suspect anything?" the director asked.

"Funny you should mention them," Stephen answered, leaning back in his chair. "Edna's on to us. And where Edna goes, Beanie follows. I'm going to meet them down at Marjorie's cottage in a few minutes. I'll try to get away with sharing as little info as I can, but you know how they are."

"Indeed, I do." The director smiled sadly. "They're two of the toughest old ladies I ever met. Would have made great agents in their heyday."

He continued. "Tell them only what you have to, Stephen. We don't want to put them in danger. Although, God help Kingpin if he tussles with those two."

William pulled a nine-millimeter pistol from his bottom desk drawer and inserted a clip. He laid the gun on his desk. "You know, Stephen, when I took the position as Magnolia director several years ago, I thought this would be a nice, relaxing job to wind down into my golden years, especially with Susan gone. I was getting bored all alone in that big house.

"I never expected to find myself smack dab in the middle of a WITSEC situation. But I have to admit, it does get the old juices going." He flashed a sly grin. "Just remember, I'm here if you need me."

Stephen felt oddly reassured, knowing his friend had his back. Something about the frumpy ex-FBI agent inspired confidence, and Stephen knew he could trust him when push came to shove.

*****

STEPHEN HAD TO WEAVE his way through the crowd packing the main hall after the morning devotion. The excited women were gawking at Brett Hopewell like teeny boppers at a Bobby Darin concert, waving lace handkerchiefs and peppering him with questions.

"Excuse me," Stephen said, gently sliding past a starry-eyed Irene Spencer. She looked him up and down, then dismissed him with a haughty sniff, preferring to stay focused on the charming Pastor Hopewell.

Stephen maneuvered his way around three abandoned walkers and two hurry-canes. Finally, he slid Miss Florrie's wheelchair a bit closer to the wall so he could slip by. She was clearly under the pastor's spell and didn't even realize she'd been moved.

Stephen smiled. *I guess no matter how old you get, some things just don't change.*

When he arrived at Marjorie's room, she opened the door on the second knock. "What? No secret code this time?" Stephen asked with a smile.

But his smile disappeared when he saw her face. "What's happened?"

"This." Marjorie shoved a crumpled piece of paper into his hand. Stephen unfolded it carefully. Written in plain block lettering on a sheet of Magnolia stationery, the note said, "That stupid cat was just the beginning."

"I found it under my door when I came back from breakfast," Marjorie said, her face white with fear. "What does it mean?"

Stephen studied the note thoughtfully. "It's a threat, Marjorie. Kingpin wants you to know he's close by, and he's not afraid to use your friends to get to you."

"So now Beanie and Edna are in danger? That's it. We've got to stop this."

Stephen pulled an envelope from his pocket, placed the

note inside, and stuck it in his pocket. "We're not going to let anything happen to you or your friends. Trust me, Marjorie. This might just be the break we've been waiting for. Kingpin knows where you are. He can come for you, but we're ready. You have your own security force watching you every minute."

Marjorie looked skeptical. "My own security force? Like who?"

"Trust me," he said with a reassuring grin. "We've got this. And soon, we'll have Kingpin behind bars."

"Not soon enough for me," Marjorie said, frowning. She headed toward the door. "Let's go. I've had enough of sitting around in this room alone, waiting for the other shoe to drop. The walls are closing in. I need a little change of scenery."

"I've got the keys to PBJ's golf cart," said Stephen, jingling the keys by their ring. "Follow me."

Instead of trying to weave their way back through Hopewell's fan club, Stephen led Marjorie down the hall toward the back of the Manor. They pushed through a heavy door that opened onto the staff parking lot. The golf cart was parked in PBJ's official space.

The morning's beautiful blue skies were now turning dark with the threat of an early afternoon storm. Soft breezes that had gently nudged the bright yellow daffodil blooms at breakfast now threatened to tear the blossoms right off their stems.

Marjorie saw sheets of rain in the distance, and big fat drops were already splattering the windshield. A sudden bolt of lightning, followed by a crashing *BOOM* of thunder, had Stephen pushing the cart to its limit, a less-than-breathtaking 20 mph.

They arrived at Marjorie's cottage just as the bottom fell out. Stephen drove straight up the driveway. The garage door opened as if by magic, thanks to a quick-thinking Beanie, who had the good sense to keep an eye out for the director's golf cart. As soon as Stephen got the cart in the garage, she pushed the automatic button to close the door behind them.

"Thanks, Beanie." Stephen smiled at the older woman. "It's truly raining cats and dogs out there." He wiped his wet face and arms with the towel Beanie handed him. "And these carts don't provide much protection."

"You two better dry off and get a move on. Edna is fit to be tied." Beanie passed Marjorie a towel. "She wants to know everything that's going on, and frankly, so do I."

Marjorie and Stephen followed Beanie through the garage to the kitchen door. The women had obviously been busy. The granite counters were covered with cardboard boxes packed full of Marjorie's possessions. One box was labeled books, another was marked clothing, and several others held knickknacks and photos. Edna stood at the sink, filling the coffee pot. She turned around when they came in.

"It's about time. Let's get this show on the road." She turned on the coffee pot and plopped down in one of Marjorie's kitchen chairs. She looked at Stephen and Marjorie expectantly.

Stephen pulled out a chair for Beanie and sat down across from Edna. Marjorie took four mugs from the kitchen cabinet while she waited for the coffee to brew. She peered around the table into the living room and was shocked by the sopping mess. Water puddled on the hardwood floors, and the upholstered sofa and chairs were covered with water stains.

"Wow, Stephen, you weren't kidding. The Chattahoochee did make a pass through here."

Beanie said, "We tried to save whatever we could. I gathered up the family pictures and mementos. I know they're irreplaceable."

Marjorie laughed dryly. "If only that were true."

Beanie looked at her quizzically.

Edna asked, "What's that supposed to mean?"

Marjorie brought the steaming mugs to the table and sat down next to Stephen. "I guess it's time to spill the beans," she said. "You tell them, Stephen."

So he did, beginning with Marjorie's unfortunate elevator ride, her stay at WITSEC, and her move to Georgia. He didn't reveal PBJ's true identity, but Edna was none too happy when he explained his own role in the situation.

"Do you mean to tell me," she exclaimed, "that you're not even a real physical therapist? No wonder my knee hurt so badly after you worked on it."

"It's OK, Edna. I've had extensive training in physical therapy. Planned on it as my career. Then I went to an on-campus recruitment meeting held by the Marshals service at Georgia State, and I was hooked." He didn't add that PBJ's dad had been there to sign him up. William had made it clear that he was only supposed to tell what he had to. PBJ's former career was on a need-to-know basis, and Beanie and Edna didn't. "But I know how to take care of your knee," he added. "I'd never hurt you."

Beanie spoke up. "Now, hold on, Edna. This is about Marjorie and her problems, not you." She frowned at her friend. "It's true Stephen isn't what he said he was, but now it's time to work together to help Marjorie."

Then Beanie did something that surprised both Marjorie and Stephen. She reached across the table and took Marjorie's hand.

"It's time to pray," she said. "We need to trust God to take control of this situation. Marjorie, He can keep you safer than Stephen and the entire Marshals service. Put your trust in Him."

"Oh, Beanie," Marjorie said, "I'm not much for religion. I mean, it's fine for you if that's what you want to believe, but it just never worked for me."

Edna took Marjorie's other hand and gave it a squeeze. "Seems like you've got nothing to lose here, sweetheart. And everything to gain."

And then Beanie closed her eyes, bowed her head, and prayed a sweet, simple prayer that touched Marjorie's heart.

"Heavenly Father, help us to be strong and courageous. To not be afraid or discouraged, no matter what danger we face, for You have promised to be with us wherever we go. Help Marjorie to trust in you with all her heart. Amen."

When she had finished praying, all four had tears in their eyes, even Stephen.

Without a word, the four friends got up from the table, rinsed their cups in the sink, and loaded Marjorie's boxes onto the back of the golf cart. Then Beanie and Edna climbed in the front seat, and Stephen and Marjorie squeezed into the back with the boxes.

The sun was shining now. The storm clouds had rolled away, and the wet grass sparkled as brightly as Edna's bedazzled cane.

After dinner that night, Beanie tapped lightly on Marjorie's door. "I have something I'd like to share with you," she said shyly. "It belonged to my sister, Nancy."

Beanie handed her a well-worn black leather Bible. Marjorie opened the cover and saw the inscription. "To Nancy, on the day of her baptism. April 24, 1956."

"Oh, Beanie. This is too precious. I can't accept it."

"Nonsense," Beanie replied. "She would want you to have it. No one enjoyed sharing her faith more than Nancy." She pressed the book into Marjorie's hands. "I'll pray that you find comfort and peace in its pages."

Marjorie placed the Bible carefully on a shelf. She didn't necessarily believe what was in it, but she respected Beanie and wouldn't do anything to hurt her feelings. So, she accepted the present, vowing to read a little every day.

Realizing she still had half an hour before lunch and nothing much to do online, Marjorie reached up and took the battered Bible from the shelf. She opened the cover and reread the inscription to Beanie's sister. She wondered what made a person want to get baptized. What did it all mean?

As she was putting the book back on the shelf, a piece of paper slipped out. Marjorie unfolded it and smoothed it out on her desk. It was some notes Beanie must have made from the Bible study the other night. She'd written in simple, straightforward script the verse John 3:16. "For God so loved the world that He gave His only Begotten Son, that whosoever believes in Him will not perish, but will have eternal life."

Marjorie's parents had taken her to church when she was little. But once she hit high school and found out Sunday school wasn't cool, she'd balked at going. And when her parents died in a car crash, she'd given up the habit altogether. How could a loving God let her parents die like that, leaving her all alone? Church and its trappings had no place in her life.

And now Beanie's trying to bring all that religion stuff back up. Well, a pie-in-the-sky God is not the answer to my problems.

Marjorie closed the Bible and shoved it back on the shelf above her desk.

Ten

Ragtime Cowgirl Irene

"*R*ight heel touch front. Tap right foot next to left. Right toe touch behind. Now bring your feet together. Repeat with your left foot. No, Alma, your other left." Beanie was barking out orders like a Broadway choreographer while John Anderson crooned "Swingin'" at full blast over the sound system.

The Raisin' Canes were going at it full force when Marjorie arrived at the Friday morning rehearsal in the recreation hall. The tables and chairs used for card games and craft lessons had been moved close to the walls, and a wooden platform had been set up for the dancers.

Marjorie pulled up a chair next to Edna. "How's it going so far? Looks like Beanie's really cracking the whip."

Edna smiled. "She knows how to keep those dancers in line, that's for sure. Comes from spending her whole life caring for five kids and a truck driver husband. She's really something, isn't she?"

Marjorie nodded. "But I see you're not going to try the dance routine. Knee just not ready to handle all that action?"

"No, it's still giving me some trouble. But Beanie assures me she has another job for me in this production. It's a surprise. Can't wait to see what she has in mind."

As if on cue, Beanie called out to her friend. "OK, Edna. Come on up here. You too, Charlie." Neither Edna nor Marjorie had seen Charlie Richardson enter the hall. But there he was. And apparently, he was to be part of the show, too.

"Bring it out, Stephen!" Beanie bellowed. Stephen opened the door to the storage closet and wheeled out Edna's surprise. A two-seater garden swing, just like the one John Anderson was singing about. Edna knew right away who was supposed to be her partner on that swing.

"Beanie, you can't be serious. You want me to swing on this thing with Charlie?" Edna was outraged. Charlie, a big grin on his face, looked quite pleased with the situation.

Beanie winked at her friend. "C'mon, Edna. It's for the Raisin' Canes. It'll spice up the show a little."

"Oh, all right," Edna conceded. "Help me up the steps, Charlie."

Like a true gentleman, Charlie extended his arm to Edna, and soon the pair were comfortably seated on the swing.

"No hanky panky, Charlie Richardson, or there will be trouble. You understand?" Edna wagged her finger in Charlie's face and used the stern voice that had quickly quieted misbehaving Sunday schoolers back in the day. That voice worked on Charlie, too. The big grin disappeared as he slid closer to his end of the swing.

Marjorie laughed at Edna's discomfort and was rewarded

with a look that could kill. That Edna was one tough cookie.

"I didn't forget about you, Marjorie," Beanie said. "Come on up here so we can teach you the routine. You'll take Edna's place, front and center."

Marjorie was horrified. "Oh, but Beanie, I'm a terrible dancer. And I don't even have a cane."

Edna piped up. "Here, Marjorie, use my cane." She flashed a self-satisfied smile at her bewildered friend. She whispered, "She who laughs last, you know."

Marjorie trudged across the stage, followed by a sparkly trail of glitter. There was no way she was going to pull this off. Maybe she could just call Kingpin and ask him to come get her right now. A better fate than having to do this dance and humiliate herself in front of all these people.

"OK, Marjorie, here we go," Beanie said. "Just keep an eye on me, and I'll show you all the steps. We'll take it a little slower until you get the hang of it. And we'll all help you. Right, girls?"

Marjorie was welcomed with lots of nods, warm smiles, and thumbs-up signs. Except for Edna. She was grinning like crazy as she swung along with Charlie.

Beanie didn't let up. "Left foot, tap. Right foot, tap. Turn to the left. Turn to the right. C'mon, Marjorie, keep up the beat."

Stephen was in the wings, keeping watch over Marjorie, as usual. He was trying to hide his amusement by covering his grin, but his shoulders shaking with laughter gave him away. Apparently, he found her lack of coordination entertaining. Marjorie sent him a look that quickly put a stop to his laughter and wiped the grin right off his face.

After an hour of Beanie's dance bootcamp, the troupe was ready for a break. As the weary dancers gathered in little groups to sip from their water bottles and munch on power bars, Beanie made a beeline to Marjorie.

"I think I need to change your position in the choreography," Beanie said, wiping her forehead with a red and white striped kerchief. She didn't meet Marjorie's eyes when she spoke, preferring instead to stare at the floor. Very un-Beanie-like.

"You sort of tower over the other dancers. Poor Alma, with her humped back, is nearly hidden by you. So, let's put you in the back row where Alma is, and we'll move her up in the front. That way, her friends and family will be able to see her. Will that be OK?"

Now, Marjorie knew the only dancer worse than her was Alma. She smiled at Beanie. "You want to hide me in the back row, right? I'm that bad, huh? Even worse than Alma? I tried to tell you, but you wouldn't listen."

Beanie's face turned bright red. She didn't want to hurt her friend's feelings, but she couldn't lie, either. "I thought with those long legs of yours and your graceful walk, you'd be a natural. 'Don't judge a book by its cover' doesn't relate just to best-selling novels, does it?"

Marjorie laughed. "I guess not. Maybe we could have a little extra practice in my room after dinner. I'm sure a little one-on-one time will make all the difference in the world."

Beanie sighed with relief, happy that her friend didn't take the criticism personally. "We'll head to your room right after dinner. You'll be dancing up a storm before you can say Grace Kelly." The friends shared a hearty laugh.

"All right, you cane raisers. Time to clear the stage to make room for the real talent in this place." Irene burst into the rec room like a Texas tornado, complete with cowgirl hat, spurs, and chaps. Her dented Walk'n Roll was decorated with a stuffed horse head and a cardboard saddle. She wore a red and white checked shirt, blue jeans, and a holster.

Marjorie stopped in her tracks. A holster?

The remaining Raisin' Canes sat down to watch the show. Marjorie pulled up a chair between Edna and Beanie.

Irene handed a CD to the sound crew and marched to the center of the stage. "Hit it, boys!" she hollered, and the intro to "Ragtime Cowboy Joe" filled the room. Irene held on to her walker and performed a gentle soft shoe routine during the first verse, sung by some nameless, long-forgotten country western group. But when it came to the chorus, Irene sang with every bit of energy she had.

What she lacked in talent, she made up for in sheer enthusiasm. And volume.

"How they run
When they hear his gun
Because the Western folks all know
He's a high-falutin', rootin', shootin'
Son of a gun from Arizona,
Ragtime Cowboy Joe."

And with that, Irene pulled a pellet gun from her holster. Yelling "Hee Haw!" she shot into the air, expecting her ammo to go up to the ceiling and fall harmlessly on the carpet. But in her excitement, her aim was off. Way off.

Charlie Richardson's glasses were the first casualty. Irene's shot bounced off the gilded frame of the treasured oil painting featuring Magnolia's founding fathers, good Baptists one and all. From there, its trajectory took it straight towards Charlie, smacking him right in the left lens. He was fine, but his glasses required immediate first aid.

At the sight of Charlie's shattered specs, the audience

panicked. Those who were able to get down on the floor hid under tables and folding chairs. The less ambulatory scrunched down in their seats and put their hands over their heads, sort of like the drills 1950s school kids did to prepare for nuclear war.

Only this wasn't a nuke. Just Irene with a toy gun and terrible aim.

Stephen rushed the stage and grabbed Irene's arm, but not before she shot another pellet into the air. This one ricocheted off the ceiling and headed toward the rec room's fancy glass door at exactly the moment PBJ stuck his head in to get a look at how the rehearsals were going. The pellet slammed into the door, shattering the glass and scaring the director half to death.

Stephen finally subdued the shooter. "Miss Irene, what were you thinking?

You could have killed someone with this thing." He took the pellet gun away from Irene and stuck it in his belt. "If you had handcuffs with that get-up, I'd put them on you and lock you up."

Irene's face glowed red hot.

Beanie climbed the stage stairs. It touched her heart to see the usually confident and brash Irene slumped down on her walker. "I was just trying to liven up the show a little," Irene said softly. "I didn't mean to hurt anyone."

"It's all right, Irene. Remember your blood pressure." Beanie was alarmed by the bright red hue of Irene's face. Everyone at the Manor knew about the older woman's high blood pressure. Beanie patted her arm. "No one really got hurt.

Director Peabody-Jones was just a little scared, and Charlie will recover quick enough. But I'm afraid his glasses are DOA.

"Let's you and me go to the dining room and get a cup of tea. That should make you feel better. And you know what?"

Beanie continued, "I think your act is terrific. Much better than ours. Of course, we're saddled with that klutzy Marjorie.

She's a beauty, for sure, but have you seen her dance?" Beanie shook her head.

"Hopeless."

Irene gave her a weak smile. "I did catch the last few minutes. Pretty awful."

Marjorie got to the stage just in time to hear the end of the conversation. Beanie gave her a wink, and Marjorie realized she was just trying to make Irene feel better. And it was true. She was a klutz. She smiled back at her friend.

Marjorie helped Stephen wheel the swing back into the storage closet. He tossed Irene's gun on a shelf. "She really could have hurt someone with that." Stephen shook his head. "I'll lock it up in here so she can't do any more damage with it."

Meanwhile, Edna walked with Charlie back to the nurse's station. He had a little scratch over his eye, and Edna wanted one of the nurses to check him out.

After she helped him to a chair in the waiting area, she went looking for Regina, Magnolia's long-suffering RN. She checked several patient rooms near the station with no luck. Finally, she headed into the medicine storage room, thinking she'd find her in there.

She was surprised to find Pearl rifling through some medicine bottles in bins on the back shelves. The bins were labeled with the names of former residents. Theodore Crumbley, John Featherstone, Gertrude Bonner. They'd all lived and died at the Manor years ago. Edna couldn't imagine why their meds were still here.

Shouldn't someone have disposed of them by now?

"What are you doing, Pearl?" Edna asked. At the sound of

Edna's voice, the cook dropped the prescription bottles she was studying and shoved the bins back on the shelves. She rushed toward the door, but Edna was right on her heels.

"Miss Beanie asked me to fetch some aspirin for Miss Irene," Pearl explained. "She said she was feeling poorly after all that mess with the gun. Did she really almost shoot the director?"

Edna smelled something fishy, and it wasn't salmon patties. "The aspirin is right here on the front counter. Everybody knows that." Edna picked up the bottle and shook two tablets into a little paper cup. "If you couldn't find them, why didn't you just wait for Regina to get back to the nurses' station?"

"Miss Beanie said to hurry, and I could tell Miss Irene had a terrible headache. I was just trying to help." She took the cup with a trembling hand.

Edna put her hand on the cook's shoulder. "Pearl, if there's something wrong, maybe I can help."

"Thank you, Miss Edna, but everything's just fine. I better get these pills to Miss Irene." Without another word, Pearl hurried down the hall.

MAGNOLIA MANOR

Eleven

Pearl's Secret

*P*astor Hopewell had joined Irene and Beanie in the dining room. All three had steaming cups of tea in front of them, and a plate of cookies sat in the middle of the table. Fully recovered from the embarrassment of a few hours earlier, Irene was smiling at the pastor and fluttering her eyelashes. Even Beanie seemed a little smitten. She laughed way too loudly at one of the pastor's jokes.

Pearl shook her head in disgust as she walked past them. She went straight into the kitchen.

Once in her office, she retrieved her purse from her desk drawer. She took the two stolen bottles of medication from her apron pocket and placed them in the side pouch before zipping it tightly. Breathing a sigh of relief, she dropped the aspirin tablets into the trash can and got to work on her famous apple dumplings, tonight's dessert.

"Well, well, Miss Pearl." The familiar voice made Pearl queasy. "I need a little more help from you."

Pearl cringed. "No. No more. You nearly killed that poor woman, and you DID kill that cat."

"Fine. Have it your way. The police will be happy to escort you off the premises. And who will supply that expensive medicine for your mom when you're behind bars?"

Pearl's shoulders slumped. She knew she was beaten. "Please. No more poison."

"Relax. You don't have to kill anyone. But I do have several jobs for you. First, you'll need to get me the key for the Manor's van. Make sure the gas tank is topped off. Next, get me the key to the landscaper's shed."

Pearl looked doubtful. "That's all? But why can't you do this yourself?"

"PBJ keeps all the keys locked up somewhere in his office. Guess he doesn't trust his staff. Ha! I wonder why," Hopewell smirked. "I don't want to take the chance of being caught rifling through the director's office. Might look suspicious."

"And it won't look suspicious for me to be seen there?" Pearl asked. "What am I supposed to say if I get caught?"

"You'll think of something. Make sure the van is parked outside the door by the recreation hall when the talent show starts. Leave the keys in the ignition. One more thing. When the Raisin' Canes finish their act, I want you to turn off the power in the entire building. You know where the circuit breaker is. You got all that?"

Pearl nodded her head.

"Good. Just remember this is the end of our deal. Get all this done right, and you'll never see me again."

He pushed open the kitchen door but stopped short when

he spotted a man nearby. "What are you doing here?" he asked, barely concealing his anger. "How long have you been standing there?"

"Oh, I'm sorry, Pastor Hopewell." Pearl recognized Charlie Richardson's voice. "I'm just looking for some coffee for me and Miss Edna. She's the sweetest lady. Took me to the nurse to get my glasses fixed and everything." He took off his glasses for Hopewell to inspect them.

Pearl knew that at one time, Charlie had been a brilliant man. A scientist, maybe? That was the rumor at the Manor. But dementia had changed all that. Now he wore a look of constant confusion and spoke like a lost child.

Hopewell pointed to the large pot in the corner of the dining room. "It's right over there," he said impatiently. "Go help yourself. I have business here with Pearl." He waited until the man walked away before retreating back into the kitchen, closing the door tightly behind him.

"Oh, I almost forgot," Hopewell said, not giving Charlie a second thought.

"Beanie and Irene were curious about why I was coming in to see you just now, so I made up a story about wanting you to bake some bread for a special communion service I'm leading tomorrow morning. Of course, I'll be long gone by then, but baking that bread will make it look like you didn't know anything about my plans. Give you sort of an alibi. And for heaven's sake, make sure it's unleavened, whatever that means."

Brett Hopewell's evil smile sent chills down Pearl's spine. If she had her wish, God would strike him dead, just like Ananias and Sapphira.

She had truly made a deal with the devil.

*****

WHILE PEARL GATHERED the ingredients for the communion bread, she thought about the mess she'd gotten herself into. That darn Cholestopine. A blessing and a curse. When the price skyrocketed, Pearl had begged the doctor for samples, talked to the pharmacists about discounts, even gone online to look for special deals. But all her research left her empty-handed.

And Mama needed that medicine. What's a daughter to do?

But then Pearl thought she'd found the answer to her prayers. At lunch one day, Beanie asked Pearl to go to the nurses' station for her. She'd forgotten to take her medicine, and she knew Regina had more if she'd just go get it so she could take it with her lunch. Pearl happily agreed. Beanie was a nice lady, down-to-earth and friendly, not like some of the snooty residents.

When Pearl got to the nurses' station, Regina was not there. She'd left the medicine closet open, an offense the director had repeatedly reprimanded her for. Pearl decided to check for Beanie's meds. Sure enough, they were right on the shelf where they were supposed to be, in a bin marked with Beanie's name.

But then, Pearl looked at the other bins. Many were labeled with names of people who were no longer residents. Alice Johnson, Carl Hopkins, Fred Romano. And as she rifled through those no-longer-used bins, she stumbled upon an unopened bottle of Cholestopine. She couldn't believe her eyes. Whether it was plain luck or God's provision, Pearl didn't know and didn't care. She glanced around to make sure no one was watching and slipped the bottle into her apron pocket.

Feeling like she'd just discovered gold, a joyful Pearl danced back to the dining room. There were literally dozens of shelves packed with past residents' medications. Surely there were many more bottles of this precious drug hiding in the forgotten bins. No one would know the difference if she helped herself.

Just to help Mama.

She returned to the closet the next day and found another bottle. The following day she found two more. And none were out of date. Pearl was thrilled.

But the next day, her luck changed. She was in the back of the closet as usual, going through past residents' bins, when out of the corner of her eye, she saw a shadow. Then the shadow spoke.

"So, Pearl, what have we here? Stealing drugs from the hands that feed you?" Brett Hopewell stood in the doorway, blocking her exit. He was smiling at her, a mean-spirited grin that frightened her.

"Hmm. I wonder how good ol' PBJ would feel about his favorite chef pushing dope?"

Pearl was terrified. "I'm not pushing dope. I'm getting these for my mother. We can't afford her medications anymore, and these weren't being used."

Hopewell put up his hand to stop her. "Tell it to the judge, Pearl. You've been caught stealing drugs from old people at the retirement home. Don't think the courts are going to look kindly on that."

As he moved closer to her, Pearl backed up until she was pressed against the back shelves. "But I can help you," he said softly. "If you're willing to help me with a few small chores."

"Like what?" Pearl whispered.

"I'm not sure, just yet. But if you keep my secrets, I'll keep yours. You do what I ask, and I won't tell the director about my little discovery. Deal?"

Pearl nodded, knowing she had no choice.

*****

WHILE THE BREAD COOLED, Pearl decided to take the bull by the horns and go find the director. She'd figure out some way to get those keys. And that would be the end of her dealings with *Pastor* Hopewell.

Pearl headed toward the recreation hall where she figured Director Peabody-Jones would be keeping an eye on the talent show practice. After all, Irene almost brought down the entire recreation hall single-handedly. He'd want to be close by in case disaster struck again.

Pearl surveyed the room quickly and zeroed in on PBJ, perched on a seat in the front row, an empty chair next to him. She made her way up the aisle and sat down.

"Hello, Miss Pearl," the director said kindly. "Everything under control for the reception after the show tonight? Hope you had time to make some of those delicious chocolate cookies I'm so fond of."

"Yes, sir. Fresh out of the oven." Pearl took a deep breath. "I need to ask a favor, though."

The director's eyes scanned the room for trouble as he answered the chef. "Of course, Pearl. What can I do for you?"

"I need to get in your office for just a second. I've made some changes to next week's menu, but I haven't had a chance to update your copy. Could you let me in for just a minute?" Pearl could feel her heart pounding, and she knew her face was as red as the pickled beets she was serving for dinner.

"I can't really leave the rehearsal right now. After all, we can't afford another disaster like Irene's. But here," he said as he reached into his jacket pocket. "Take my office key and do what you need to do. Bring it back when you're finished."

He handed her the key without taking his eyes off the stage.

"Thanks, Director. I wanted to ask you if I could borrow the van for a few minutes, too," she asked in a calm voice. "I need to pick up some items for the reception after the show. I won't be long."

"That's fine, Pearl. You'll find the key in my right-hand drawer. Just put the key back when you're finished with it. And bring me my office key. I'm sure I'll still be here. That Irene Spencer is going to be the death of me," he mumbled.

Pearl scooted down the aisle, the key clenched tightly in her hand. When she made it through the door to the hallway, she broke into a full-out run, something she hadn't tried in years. She was pleasantly surprised at her speed.

She rounded the corner to the director's office and slowed as she passed the lobby and the front office. Since it was Saturday, the staff had the day off, so no one was there to see what she was doing. What would it matter anyway? PBJ had given his permission.

She pulled the director's keys from her pocket. Three keys on a simple ring. Two small, one large. She slid the large key into the lock on the office door, and it opened easily.

Pearl flipped on the light and quietly closed the door behind her. Next week's menu was still in his IN basket where she'd left it yesterday morning. She found a pen on top of his desk and crossed out a few items on the menu. No blueberry muffins on Tuesday, ice cream instead of banana pudding on Friday, as long as the ice cream man didn't get stuck under the bridge again, and fried chicken instead of pork chops on Saturday.

Now she'd just have to remember to make all those changes on her own copy. Not like PBJ would notice. As long as he got fried chicken, he'd be happy.

She tried one of the small keys in the lock on the director's desk and was surprised when it worked. Pearl opened the right-hand drawer, and after rifling through an assortment of pens, paper clips, and post-it notes, she found the van key and slid it into her pocket. Deeper in the drawer, she found a key labeled "shed" and dropped that in her pocket, too.

She should have stopped right there, locked up the drawer, and slipped out the office door. But her curiosity, what her Mama called just plain nosiness, got the better of her. Did frumpy old PBJ have secrets of his own?

She opened each of the drawers carefully, not wanting to displace anything. Pearl didn't want to leave any clues that she'd been poking around his desk. Everything seemed pretty normal, messy but normal, until she opened the bottom right drawer and found the gun. Her jaw dropped.

"What in the world?" Her voice was loud in the empty room, and it startled her. Along with the gun, she saw a framed certificate with enormous gold lettering:

Federal Bureau of Investigation.
This letter of commendation is presented to special agent William Peabody-Jones for exemplary service to his country.

Pearl shook her head in amazement. You just never knew about people.

She slid the frame back into its place in the drawer. Next, she reached for the gun and turned it over in her hand, surprised by its weight. Pearl had always been fascinated by guns, even as a little girl. Her daddy had one he kept locked in a safe in the bedroom closet. Even taught her to use it. He was proud of what a good shot she was.

Pearl considered what to do next. Finally, she took the gun and some ammunition and hid them in her pocket. She locked the desk up tight, turned off the light, and slipped out the door. She patted her pocket to be sure she had the keys — and the gun — tucked safely inside.

Now she had to gas up the van and park it by the rehearsal hall door. After that, she'd find the circuit breaker so she could turn off the lights at the right time. And then, if all went according to plan, she'd be finished with Hopewell once and for all.

Twelve

Just-A-Swingin'

When Marjorie arrived for the dress rehearsal, the performances were in full swing. Marjorie was surprised to see that the room looked no worse for wear after Irene's one-woman demolition derby yesterday. Maintenance crews had cleaned up the shattered glass and replaced the door. The spot that once held the portrait of Magnolia's founding fathers now featured a cheap Walmart copy of Da Vinci's "Starry Night." It would do until the founding fathers could be properly reframed and placed back in their position of honor.

Marjorie and Stephen went to the storage closet to get the swing ready for the show. While they were in there, Irene's gun, hidden on a shelf, caught Stephen's eye. He just couldn't resist getting another look at it.

"This thing looks almost real," he said, hefting Irene's gun in his hand.

"She's lucky the police didn't put her away." Stephen tucked the gun between the Christmas decorations and a plastic Thanksgiving turkey. "I'll get rid of this after the show." Then he and Marjorie slid the swing out of the closet and parked it up against the wall so it would be ready when the Raisin' Canes needed it.

The rehearsal opened with the Magnolia choir, directed by Pastor Hopewell, singing his foot-tapping version of "I'll Fly Away." He thoroughly beguiled the ladies in the audience with his mastery of the ivories and his handsome smile.

Next, popular resident Terry Ellington, no relation to Duke, brought down the house with his rousing rendition of "Chattanooga Choo Choo." He was followed by the lovely O'Connor twins, Nancy and Patty, who were on the cusp of their ninety-ninth birthday. They had the audience singing along with their snappy arrangement of "Yellow Submarine" played on dueling autoharps. Retired schoolteacher Gail Joiner, who'd always dreamed of being a concert pianist, brought a little culture to the show by impressing the rather low-brow audience with her interpretation of Debussy's "Claire de Lune."

As the time drew near for the Raisin' Canes to take the stage, Beanie's nerves started to show, and she took it out on her dancers.

"Ethyl, fold up the cuffs of those blues jeans twice, not just once. You look like something straight off the farm."

"Helen, can't you get those tennis shoes whiter? I know you're having trouble with cataracts, dear, but really, we don't want to look slovenly."

"Roberta, that gingham shirt is the wrong shade of red. See if you can find another one in the storage closet."

With half the dance troupe in tears and the other half ready to pummel Beanie with their canes, Marjorie knew it was time to take action. "Beanie, you've got to calm down. This is just the dress rehearsal," she said as she walked her friend to the refreshment table. She poured a glass of punch. "Here, drink this. Now take a deep breath. The show is going to be fine." She patted Beanie on the shoulder.

Marjorie said, "I'll get a shirt for Roberta. You go back and be nice to your dancers. They could turn on you at any minute, and remember, they're armed. Those canes could be classified as deadly weapons."

Beanie smiled. "Guess I have been a little bossy. Usually, Edna keeps me in check, but she's gone to get Rebecca. Such a sweet girl. She's volunteered to help with our makeup and hair for the show tonight."

"Just hang in there until Edna gets back." She patted Beanie on the shoulder.

"Everything's going to be fine. I've even learned my steps."

And then the raucous notes of "Swingin'" filled the rehearsal hall, and the Raisin' Canes took the stage. For Marjorie, it was sheer magic. For a few short minutes, while she lost herself in the dance, she forgot all about Kingpin and his threats. Instead, she found herself enjoying the beat of the music and the appreciative clapping of the audience. Beanie beamed at her progress.

But then Stephen had to ruin her good mood with very bad news. He took her arm as she stepped down from the platform. "The FBI contacted me. They have a lead on Kingpin's hitman. They're convinced he's close by, maybe even here in the Manor. Keep your eyes peeled, OK?"

Marjorie's whole body trembled. "It might be somebody here? But, Stephen, do you have any idea who it could be?" She looked around nervously.

He shook his head. "No, so until he makes his move, we're going to stick together like white on rice. Got it?"

Marjorie smiled weakly at the old-fashioned expression. "But what if we catch him? I mean, isn't Kingpin still going to be after me? If I testify, he'll go to prison."

"Not if we can coerce the hitman to turn on his boss. Rat out his whole organization. Give us Kingpin's location. And with the charges he'll be facing, he'd be a fool not to take a deal. When we have Kingpin, you'll be free and clear."

But both Marjorie and Stephen wondered if that day would ever come.

By five o'clock that afternoon, the Raisin' Canes were relaxing in their rooms, enjoying a box dinner of tasty chicken salad, a freshly baked croissant, and a delicious chocolate chip cookie.

Edna was back at the Manor with Rebecca in tow. The young girl got right to work on her grandmother's makeup and hairdo. Edna sat on a little bench in front of her antique dressing table and watched her granddaughter go to work.

"OK, Nana, we're almost finished. Just a little more eyeliner." Rebecca stuck her tongue between her teeth as she concentrated on Edna's face. "There. You look perfect."

Edna eyed herself in the mirror. "Girl, you're a miracle worker. Where'd you learn to do makeup like this? I look twenty years younger."

"Ah, Nana, it's easy, really. I watched a YouTube video. It says it's all about bringing out your inner beauty to make your outsides look beautiful. Or something like that." She paused as she sprayed Edna's hair in place. "Besides, you're already gorgeous on the inside. I just coaxed it out a little."

Edna beamed at her in the mirror. "Well, now comes the real challenge. See if you can coax some of Beanie's beauty out of her heart and onto her face. No one is more beautiful on the inside than Beanie, but she's not one to spend time on makeup and hairspray. You may have a fight on your hands."

Rebecca smiled. "Oh, I love Beanie. She won't fight me. It'll be fun." Rebecca's face turned serious. "There is something I need to talk to you about, though, Nana."

Hearing the sincerity in Rebecca's voice, Edna turned in her chair so she could sit eye to eye with her granddaughter. "What is it, Rebecca?"

The girl gave Edna a shy smile. "I want to get baptized at church tomorrow, Nana."

Tears filled Edna's eyes. "Oh, sweetheart, that's wonderful! I'm so proud of you!"

"There's one more thing, Nana," Rebecca said softly. "You have been such a big part of me learning about Jesus. You always made sure I went to Sunday school, even when Mom and Dad couldn't take me. And you dragged me to Vacation Bible School even though I wanted to go swimming with my friends instead." She let out a little laugh. "And you came to all those awful choir programs I've been in every year since I was two."

Edna took hold of her granddaughter's hands. "It's been a privilege to be a part of your life, Rebecca. To watch you grow and mature has brought me so much joy. Someday you'll understand when you have a granddaughter of your own. Now, what's the one more thing?"

"Nana, will you baptize me? I know your knee bothers you sometimes, and it might be hard for you to get into the baptistery, but Dad will help you. And Mom and Dad already talked to Pastor Romans to make sure he wouldn't mind."

Edna could barely speak around the boulder-sized lump that had formed in her throat. Tears flowed freely now. It took her a moment before she could answer.

"I'd be honored, Rebecca."

The girl threw her arms around her grandmother and hugged her tightly. "Thanks, Nana. Pastor Romans will be there to answer any questions you have. But you have to stop crying! I'm going to have to do your makeup all over again."

Edna replied, "Oh, but Rebecca, these are such happy tears. I love you, sweet girl." Edna squeezed her so hard, the girl could barely breathe. But she gave her Nana a big smile anyway.

Thirteen

Taking a Mulligan

$\mathcal{R}$ebecca quickly gathered her beauty supplies and then pulled her cellphone from her back pocket to check the time. "Yikes! Looks like I better move on to Beanie's room if I'm going to get everyone ready in time for the show. I still have two Raisin' Canes to do after her."

With supplies in hand, the girl rushed out the door without looking for oncoming traffic in the hallway. To Rebecca's horror, lipsticks, blush, brushes, and hairspray went airborne as she collided with Stephen and Marjorie in Edna's doorway. A light layer of face powder floated down the hall like a pink cloud.

"Oops!" a red-faced Rebecca mumbled as she bent down to pick up her supplies. "So sorry. I'm in a hurry to get the rest of the dance group ready for their big number, and I wasn't paying attention to where I was going."

Marjorie laughed. "No worries, Rebecca. You are Rebecca, right? I'm Marjorie, and this is Stephen, your grandmother's physical therapist."

She stuck out her hand to shake Marjorie's. Then she shook Stephen's. "I'm sorry for running into you. But I'm on my way to Beanie's room to do her makeup, and she can be a little prickly sometimes." Rebecca smiled. "But she's my second favorite grandmother."

"It's nice to meet you, Rebecca," said Stephen, giving her a big smile. Then he turned to Edna. "I have some errands to take care of before the show tonight. I'm just dropping Marjorie off to visit with you for a little while." He gave Edna a serious look that the older woman understood immediately. It clearly said, "Keep an eye on Marjorie."

As he walked away, three pairs of eyes followed him down the hall.

Edna sighed. "He is a nice-looking man."

"Nana! I'm shocked!" said Rebecca with a grin. "He is kind of cute, though. For an old guy. He'd be just right for you, Marjorie."

Marjorie playfully punched the young girl in the shoulder. "That's enough out of you, Miss Rebecca."

Rebecca smiled and took off down the hall in a burst of energy and a haze of hairspray to tackle Beanie's makeup.

"Youth is wasted on the young," bemoaned Edna. "Oh, to have a third of that get-up and go."

Marjorie said, "And to have your whole life ahead of you." She shook her head sadly. "Some days, I wish I could have a mulligan on the past sixty years. Start fresh, you know?"

Edna closed the door and motioned for Marjorie to sit down at her little dining table. The table was covered with a hand-embroidered linen cloth that Marjorie knew must be an heirloom. Delicate white china cups and saucers sat at the ready. A soft breeze ruffled the lovely lace curtains decorating Edna's windows, and an ivory bedspread on her four-poster bed made Edna's room inviting and comforting. Marjorie took a deep breath and felt herself relax.

The coffee pot gurgled and spewed steam from a nearby counter. Edna poured two cups of coffee and sat down across from her friend. "Suppose I told you a mulligan's out there with your name on it just waiting for you to claim it?"

Marjorie looked puzzled. "What do you mean? I can't start my life over. What's done is done, and I just have to live with it."

Edna got her Bible from the bedside table. Her heart fluttered a little, and her hands were sweaty. Even though she'd been a Christian for decades, talking to people about Jesus had always been her husband's territory. She was just the preacher's wife. Suppose she said the wrong thing, and Marjorie turned away from God because of her?

After a quick silent prayer that the Holy Spirit would guide her words, Edna dove in.

She patted Marjorie's hand. "God is not through with you, dear friend. You don't think that maybe, just maybe, the bullet in that elevator missed you for a reason? Or Mr. Whiskers ate that poison instead of you? Oh, you can say they're both coincidences, and maybe you're right. But suppose God's protecting you because He has a purpose for you. I want to tell you a story about a woman in the Bible who really needed a mulligan, and Jesus gave it to her. Look here."

Edna opened her Bible to the book of John, chapter 8. "In this story, Jesus has gone to the temple to teach the people. The

Pharisees — they're sort of like the temple leadership — brought in a woman who had been caught in the act of adultery. And the Pharisees said to Jesus, 'In the Law, Moses commanded us to stone such a woman. What do you say?'"

Marjorie gasped. "That's terrible. What did Jesus do?"

"Well, He bent down and started to write in the dirt with his finger. They kept on questioning Him until He straightened up and said to them, 'Let any of you without sin be the first to throw a stone at her.' Then He bent down and started writing again."

"What was He writing?" Marjorie asked, clearly caught up in the story.

"No one knows for sure, but some Bible scholars think He might have been writing the names of the Pharisees or maybe the sins they committed. But listen to what happens." Edna was as excited to finish the story as Marjorie was.

"The Pharisees began to go away one at a time, the older ones first, until only Jesus was left with the woman still standing there," Edna read aloud. "Then Jesus straightened up and asked her, 'Woman, where are they? Has no one condemned you?"

"No one, sir," she said.

"Then neither do I condemn you," Jesus declared. "Go now and leave your life of sin."

Edna looked up to see Marjorie's eyes damp with tears. "How's that for a mulligan?" the older woman asked. "Marjorie, the Bible is full of stories like this one. Jesus can wipe your slate clean and let you start all over again. All you have to do is ask." She patted Marjorie's hand, and the younger woman wiped away her tears.

A knock on the door brought them both down to earth.

Rebecca burst into the room. She looked from her Nana's

smiling face to Marjorie's tears. She was puzzled but decided to mind her own business. This time.

"Hey, Marjorie, I thought I'd find you here. I'm finished dolling up the other Raisin' Canes. It's your turn if you're interested. And, Nana, I brought some extra glitter for your cane. I want it all blinged out for the show tonight."

"But your Nana's not dancing tonight, Rebecca. I am," Marjorie moaned. "And if that cane is any more 'blinged' out, I'll never be able to hide. I'll stand out like a really glittery sore thumb."

"Oh, Miss Marjorie, you'll look beautiful no matter what."

"You haven't seen her dance, dear," Edna whispered in her granddaughter's ear.

"Nana! That wasn't very nice!" Rebecca was shocked.

"It's fine," Marjorie said. "She's right. I'm terrible."

Rebecca laughed. "Maybe this will help then." She pulled glue and glitter out of her pocket and bedazzled Edna's cane. As she laid out her makeup on Edna's dresser, she asked, "Did Nana tell you she's going to baptize me tomorrow at my church?"

"Why, no, she didn't. That's wonderful, Rebecca." Marjorie smiled at the young girl, but Edna noticed the flash of doubt in her eyes.

"Tell Marjorie why you want to be baptized, dear," Edna urged Rebecca.

"Oh, that's simple," the girl replied as she brushed Marjorie's hair. "Jesus loves me so much He died to take away my sins. I want Him to be in charge of my life."

She put down the brush and stared at Marjorie in the mirror. "I have a great idea! Would you like to come to see me get baptized? It'd be awesome to have you there. Do you think

Beanie would come, too?"

In a flash, Rebecca was out the door and on her way to Beanie's room, leaving a shocked Marjorie holding the hairbrush. The girl was back in an instant, a big grin spreading across her face.

"She said yes! All my favorite people will be there for me. I'm so excited I just can't wait!"

Twenty minutes later, with her hair and makeup complete, Marjorie had to admit she looked pretty good, maybe even beautiful.

"Thanks, Rebecca," she said, turning her head from right to left to check out her new look. "You made me look like a queen instead of the clumsy Raisin' Cane relegated to the back row."

Rebecca threw her arms around Marjorie and squeezed. "You'd look beautiful no matter what. But you need to get changed into your costume. Want me to go with you and help you get ready?"

"No, you stay here and help Edna. I'll get dressed and be back in a few minutes."

She gave Edna a quick smile before quietly closing the door. Her heart felt light as she dashed across the hall to her room. At least it did before she opened her door and saw the intruder waiting inside.

Fourteen

The Show Must Go On

"*H*ello, Marjorie."

She instantly recognized the smooth-as-silk voice. Brett Hopewell.

What was he doing here?

Her visitor continued. "I'm confused, my dear. Am I speaking to Marjorie Riley? Or perhaps your real name is Marjorie Sims?"

Marjorie gasped. "How did you find me?" She backed away, but not fast enough.

Brett Hopewell moved quickly to her door, blocking her exit. He grabbed her from behind, wrapped one arm around her waist, and pressed his other hand against her mouth.

"Never put anything online that you don't want the world to see. Remember when Kristina took your picture in the dining room? Kingpin's tech people found it within hours, and now, here I am."

Marjorie struggled to get away but found she couldn't move.

She felt his hot breath on the back of her neck. "Now, don't make a sound," he whispered. "I'm going to take my hand away, and I need for you to stay absolutely quiet. There's more at stake here than you know. Like the lives of your little-old-lady friends, Edna and Beanie. Are you ready to listen?"

Marjorie nodded, her eyes wide with fear.

"Good. I thought you'd cooperate. Now, sit down over there." He released her and pointed to the bed. "Time for us to have a little talk. But first, go put this on." Hopewell tossed her costume to her, and Marjorie ducked into the bathroom to change as quickly as possible.

How am I going to get out of this mess?

*****

From his vantage point on the dirt floor, Stephen stretched his neck to peer through the shed's grimy window. The duct tape on his mouth made it impossible to call for help.

His hands and feet were bound with duct tape, too, and he was hogtied with a thick piece of rope. He felt like a helpless calf in a Texas rodeo. Ants were having a picnic on his right leg, and his head felt like it had been beaten with a hammer.

He tried to remember how he'd gotten in this situation.

He recalled leaving Marjorie at Edna's room. He'd had a meeting scheduled with PBJ, but Brett Hopewell had met him in the hall. The details were sketchy in Stephen's mind, but he remembered Hopewell saying something about finding important evidence, and he'd wanted Stephen to investigate.

Stephen remembered walking with him to the shed. But everything went black when he followed Hopewell around the corner.

Someone must have come up from behind and smacked him in the head hard enough to knock him out. Now glancing around the shed, he saw a blood-smeared tire iron on the floor a few feet away. The weapon of choice.

So, obviously, Hopewell had lured him there to get him away from Marjorie.

He is definitely Kingpin's man. But who's his tire-iron-wielding accomplice?

And who's protecting Marjorie?

Stephen struggled to free his hands and feet. No luck. He had to get to Marjorie. Because without his protection, she didn't stand a chance.

*****

HOPEWELL PRESSED HIS HAND into the small of her back as he walked her down the hall toward the recreation room.

He whispered in her ear. "Now, remember. Just do as I told you, and your friends will be fine."

Marjorie nodded. She tried to stay calm, thinking about how it would help Edna and Beanie. One false move by her and Hopewell would kill them.

"You saw how easy it was to kill off Irene Spencer's cat. No one even had me on their radar screen as a suspect. Just think how simple it would be for me to rid the world of those two old women."

"Where's Stephen?" Marjorie asked softly, trying to get him to change the subject. She didn't want to think about Edna and Beanie getting hurt because of her.

"He's not your concern anymore."

Marjorie shivered. She had no choice. She would do exactly as he said to protect her friends. She didn't know a lot about prayer, but this seemed like a good time to get started. Her lips moved silently as she continued down the hallway with Hopewell.

The recreation hall was packed with friends and relatives. The room hummed with excitement as the performers took their places. Brett Hopewell, still playing the gracious gentleman, steered Marjorie to a chair between Edna and Beanie.

"So sorry I have to leave you girls to go direct my choir, but I'll be back." He squeezed Marjorie's shoulder and flashed her a smile that caused bile to rise in her throat.

Beanie cringed at his use of the word 'girls.' Even though he said it with that smooth voice of his, it still came out as an insult.

Edna ignored it, too, and pressed on to more important matters. "What's that all about? Don't tell me you've snatched Pastor Hopewell off the singles shelf? There will be an awful lot of disappointed women at Magnolia Manor. So how did it happen?" Edna leaned close to Marjorie. She didn't want to miss a word.

"Yes," Beanie chimed in. "Give us all the details."

Marjorie replied coolly, "Oh, the ladies have nothing to worry about. We're just friends. There's nothing romantic about us at all."

Edna and Beanie looked at their friend quizzically, but they didn't have time for more questions. They'd have to get all the dirt later. The show was about to start.

The crowd enthusiastically clapped for each and every act. Even Irene got a generous round of applause for her "Ragtime Cowboy Joe" number, made safer but not as entertaining by the absence of gunfire.

In order to get the stage ready, a brief intermission was scheduled before the Raisin' Canes performed. Marjorie's palms were sweaty, and her heart was racing. Hopewell's instructions echoed in her head. "When your dance is finished, the lights all over the building are going to go out. I'll be at the back of the stage. You'll follow me out the door where the van will be waiting. And remember, not a word to anyone."

"Marjorie, have you heard anything I said?" Edna's panic-tinged voice shook Marjorie from her thoughts. "Have you seen Charlie? I'll be swinging on that swing by myself if he doesn't get here in a minute." She wrung her hands nervously. "And where's Stephen? Who's going to help you move the swing?"

"I can wheel the swing out of the closet myself, but I'll need some help getting it onto the stage," Marjorie replied. "I haven't seen Charlie or Stephen.

Don't know where they could be. You weren't that crazy about swinging with Charlie anyway, were you?"

"No, I suppose not," Edna replied grimly, "but it's better than being an old-maid single swinger. Darn him. I can't believe he'd ditch me. Again."

A red-faced Beanie, in full panic mode, rushed over to them. "Marjorie," she ordered, "get the swing out of the closet. I'll find someone to help you get it on the platform."

She turned her attention to Edna. "PBJ agreed to be your partner on the swing. So, let's go, ladies! Get a move on!"

Fifteen

What's Up with PBJ?

$\mathcal{M}$arjorie flipped on the light in the storage closet. She pulled on the swing but couldn't budge it. Something was blocking the wheels. She bent over to have a look and saw Irene's pellet gun that nearly blinded poor Charlie Richardson. It must have fallen from the shelf.

She picked it up and quickly slid it in the waistband of her jeans and pulled her vest over it. Stephen had said it looked genuine enough to fool the police.

Maybe it would even fool Brett Hopewell.

"I'll be happy to give you a hand with the swing." Marjorie jumped a foot off the ground when she heard his voice. Hopewell wore a wicked grin as he grabbed the other end of the swing. They rolled it to the stage.

Beanie breathed a sigh of relief. "OK, we're ready to go. Places everyone. Director, you sit there by Edna." PBJ smiled at

Edna as he sat down.

The Raisin' Canes lined up, and Beanie signaled to the audio booth to start the music. The ladies beamed as the crowd clapped along with the familiar tune, "And we were swingin'." PBJ and Edna made a cute couple as they waved from their perch on the swing.

Marjorie pasted a fake smile on her face. She'd do anything to protect her friends, even if it meant going along with Hopewell's scheme. She danced as she'd never danced before, hoping against hope Stephen would show up.

Where could he be? Marjorie wondered as the music drew to a close.

And then the lights went out.

*****

STEPHEN HEARD THE GOLF CART approaching and saw its lights flickering through the window. Then footsteps, running toward him. Finally, the old wooden door splintering as Charlie Richardson, retired U.S. Marshal, burst in. The beam of his flashlight lit up the shed.

"Stephen, are you all right?" Charlie ripped the tape off Stephen's mouth. He pulled a knife out of his pocket and sawed away at the ropes.

"Yeah, I'm OK," Stephen said, rubbing his wrists. "It's Hopewell. He's Kingpin's hitman. But there's someone helping him. Hopewell got me down here with a cockamamie story about evidence here in the shed, but somebody else came up behind me and hit me in the head. Knocked me out.

"We've got to get to Marjorie," Stephen exclaimed as he got to his feet. He touched his head gingerly and saw the blood on his fingers. "You better drive, Charlie. I'm seeing two of you right now, and that can't be a good sign."

Charlie helped his former partner get in the golf cart and started the engine.

It whined pitifully as Charlie revved it up.

"How did you know I was in the shed?" Stephen asked as Charlie cruised along the path at the max speed of twenty miles per hour.

"I was standing by the kitchen door and overheard Hopewell talking to Pearl. He said he needed the keys to the van and the shed, and she would be free of him if she got them for him. Oh, and there was something about turning off all the lights, too."

Stephen nodded. "You're really making this phony dementia work for you, aren't you? No one suspects you're a retired marshal. But couldn't you have found a decent set of wheels?" Stephen slapped the dashboard. "Can't you get this thing to go faster?"

"Like the getaway we made through Death Valley in that souped-up Jeep? That was awesome." Charlie smiled as he remembered. "You really had a thing for that beautiful blonde we were protecting."

"Hey, let's talk about you and Miss Edna. I've seen how you look at her. Not part of your dementia act, either," Stephen shot back.

Charlie grinned sheepishly and pushed the cart to go even faster.

Stephen pointed ahead. "Look, all the lights are out in the Manor. Did you hear anything else about Hopewell's plans?"

"Nope, that was it. But I say we look for the van. That's got to be part of his exit strategy." Charlie made a hard left and headed for the rehearsal hall parking lot.

"Aha!" Charlie said when he spied the van near the door, its lights off but the engine running. He stopped the golf cart behind a hedge of holly bushes and turned off the motor.

Charlie and Stephen crept through the darkness to the passenger side of the van. A quick sweep with Charlie's flashlight showed no one inside. Stephen opened the door, climbed in, and turned off the engine, depositing the keys in his pocket.

They returned to their hiding place in the bushes and waited. In the darkness, they could just make out two figures emerging from the recreation hall door.

"Hopewell and Marjorie!" Stephen whispered. "Let's get them."

Charlie grabbed his arm. "Wait. You said he has an accomplice. Let's see who it is."

The two men watched as Hopewell forced Marjorie toward the van. Then, realizing the van wasn't running, Hopewell pulled open the driver's side door. He slammed Marjorie up against the van and held her there while he frantically searched the floorboards by the light of the dim overhead bulb.

"Why doesn't she run?" asked Stephen, perplexed. "Why is she just standing there?"

"Because Hopewell's got something on her," Charlie replied. "Look."

Stephen saw PBJ standing at the door, a flashlight in his hand. The director pushed Edna and Beanie toward the van. "What are you doing? Why isn't the van running?" PBJ shot the flashlight at Hopewell's face.

"Somebody took the keys," Hopewell answered, his anger about to boil over.

"What are you doing with those two?" He pointed his gun at Beanie and Edna.

"They were looking for her," said PBJ, motioning at Marjorie.

"They were afraid something bad had happened to her when the lights went out and they couldn't find her." PBJ frowned. "Seems they were right."

"Great," Hopewell said. "Now what are we going to do? So much for an easy getaway." He studied PBJ for a minute. "Where's your gun, anyway? Three old women aren't going to put up a fight, but you might need a weapon if push comes to shove, if you catch my drift." He motioned at the frightened women.

"Someone took it from my desk drawer. Thought it was locked up, but guess I was wrong. And like you said, these three won't put up a fight. Will you, girls?"

Under the circumstances, Beanie decided to let the word 'girls' pass without comment.

But she had a plan.

"The ice cream truck's over by the kitchen door," Beanie said quietly. "Pearl ordered extra sherbet for the punch tonight, and the delivery boy just got here a few minutes ago."

At first, Edna was confused by Beanie's comment. Then, after she gave it a little thought, she shot her friend a sly smile.

"And the delivery boy always leaves the engine running so the ice cream won't melt," Edna added.

"What are you two doing? Why are you trying to help them?" Marjorie had no idea what her friends were up to.

"Shut up, all of you." Hopewell turned to PBJ. "All right. We'll have to take them with us and let Kingpin deal with them." He shoved the gun into Beanie's back. "The ice cream truck it is. Let's go. Ladies first."

Beanie led the way down the narrow path, with Marjorie and Edna close behind. PBJ lit the trail with his flashlight while Hopewell kept the women in line with his gun.

And behind them, close enough to see what was happening, were Stephen and Charlie.

Beanie rounded the corner of the building and stopped short. "There it is," she said, "just like I told you." The box truck was parked near the kitchen door, and the engine was running. The back door of the truck was open, and the driver was nowhere to be seen.

"Time to go for a ride, ladies. It may be a little chilly back here, but you'll have all the ice cream you can eat. Get in." Hopewell motioned with his gun.

Edna tried to reason with him. "Pastor Hopewell, there's no need to do this. Beanie and I really aren't of any use to you. We don't know anything about Kingpin."

"That's right," Beanie chimed in. "And I'm sure Marjorie wouldn't say a word about the detective's murder and...."

"Beanie!" Edna squeezed her friend's arm hard to make her stop talking.

"Ouch! That hurt!" Beanie rubbed the spot. "I was just trying to help."

"You did help, Miss Beanie," Hopewell said in his whiskey-smooth voice. "Now that I know you and Edna have heard the whole story, Kingpin will be glad I brought you along for the ride. Now get in."

PBJ pushed Edna and Beanie into the truck, but Marjorie had had enough. "Hopewell, our deal was I'd go with you to Kingpin, but you'd leave my friends alone. They have nothing to do with this. Let them go."

"Marjorie, surely you're not that naive. My job is to tie up all of Kingpin's loose ends. And I've got three right here that I'm about to take care of." He was tired of arguing. "Get in before I shoot all of you."

Marjorie reluctantly climbed into the truck. PBJ closed the doors, but before he locked them in, he tossed in his flashlight.

"Here," he said. "I'm really not all bad."

"Prove it by letting us go," Marjorie shot back.

"No can do, my dear." He slammed the doors shut.

Marjorie heard the rattling of chains being wound around the door handles and the loud click of a padlock being closed. She sank down to her knees. "I'm so sorry I got you both into this," she said. "I didn't want either of you to get hurt, and now look." She scanned the back of the truck with the flashlight. "We're going to be shot by Kingpin if we don't freeze to death first."

"Marjorie, don't worry. We have a plan." Beanie and Edna smiled in the semi-darkness as they filled Marjorie in on all the details.

*****

THE DELIVERY BOY RAN out the kitchen door just in time to see his truck disappear down the driveway. He pulled out his cellphone to call 911 but realized he had no service. "Never works back here," he groused. "How can people live in a place without a cellphone?"

Charlie and Stephen heard him yelling at Pearl to dial 911 as they ran back to the van. Stephen pulled the van keys from his pocket and jammed them in the ignition.

A sudden banging on the side of the van startled both men. Stephen looked out his rearview mirror and saw Pearl standing there, a gun in her hand.

"What are you doing?" he yelled as he opened the door.

"Let me in. I'm going with you," Pearl replied. "This mess is mostly my fault, but I'll explain that later." She showed him the gun. "I know how to use this. And you can use all the help you can get."

"Where'd you get the gun?" Charlie asked, all signs of dementia gone.

Pearl studied him up and down. "Charlie Richardson? Guess none of us are who we seem to be, huh?"

She answered his question. "PBJ gave me his office keys so I could get Hopewell the keys to the shed and the van. I found the gun in the director's desk drawer. Thought it might come in handy tonight. Now let me in before I shoot out your tires."

Stephen shrugged. "Fine. Get in. But I warned you."

They drove down the long driveway from the Manor at breakneck speed. "I don't see them anywhere," Charlie said. "How fast can an ice cream truck go?"

"I think I know where we'll find them," Pearl said. "Just stay on this road, and we'll catch up with them shortly."

Stephen and Charlie both shook their heads. "Whatever you say, Miss Pearl," said Charlie with a grin.

Sixteen

The Power of Butter Pecan

"*I*'ll hit PBJ with my cane. Beanie, you start throwing half gallons of ice cream at Hopewell as soon as those doors open. Marjorie, you help her." Edna was in full-on Sunday school teacher mode, ready to fight the good fight and defend her friends. Marjorie was sure Edna was working up to a chorus of "Onward, Christian Soldiers."

Beanie added her two cents. "I guess if David can take down Goliath with a smooth stone, I can take down Hopewell with a carton of vanilla fudge."

"I might be able to do more than pelt them with frozen goodies," Marjorie said. She pulled Irene's pellet gun from her waistband.

Beanie and Edna gasped. "How'd you get that thing past Hopewell?" asked Edna.

"He never thought to frisk me. He sees me as an old woman,

no threat to him."

"Ha! This might be kind of fun!" remarked Beanie. When Marjorie and Edna looked at her as if she'd lost her mind, she quickly added, "If we don't get killed, that is."

But Marjorie suddenly got very quiet. "Did I ever tell you two about my claustrophobia?" she asked quietly. In her mind, the walls of the small truck seemed to be moving in closer, preparing to smother her. Despite the cold temperatures in the ice cream truck, her fear caused her to break out in a sweat.

Edna and Beanie put their arms around their friend. "Oh, no," said Beanie. "Try not to think about it, Marjorie. Want some ice cream? I think I saw some mint chocolate chip around here somewhere."

"Normally, I'd be all over that," Marjorie said with a weak smile. "But right now, the only thing that would help is opening those doors."

The three women huddled against the frozen wall of the ice cream truck, bumping along the deserted country road. With their arms around each other for warmth and emotional support, they prayed and waited. And prayed some more.

Suddenly, with an ear-splitting screech that rivaled Irene's shrieky high note, the truck came to a violent stop, sending the women sliding into crates of ice cream.

"Ladies, I believe we have arrived at our destination," Edna announced as she took hold of a large crate to pull herself up. "Like a plug in a barrel."

Marjorie was confused. "What are you talking about?"

Beanie quickly explained. "Hopewell hasn't been here long enough to know this road leads through an underpass that's too low for the ice cream truck to get through. PBJ probably just forgot. Or Hopewell wouldn't listen. Anyway, the truck is now jammed in so tight it can't move forward or backward."

Marjorie's eyes went wide at the sound of the padlock being opened.

"It is wide enough to walk around the sides, though," Beanie added glumly.

Edna jumped in. "Gird your loins, ladies. Time for the attack." She swung her cane up over her shoulder like she was Freddie Freeman, up at-bat for the Atlanta Braves at the bottom of the ninth.

Encouraged by Edna's spunky attitude, Marjorie aimed Irene's gun bravely and prepared to shoot at whatever opened that door. Oh, what she wouldn't do for her can of MaceFace.

Beanie planted her feet firmly on the floor of the truck. She held a frozen carton of mint chocolate chip in one hand and a tub of butter pecan in the other.

"The nuts might give it an extra oompf," she explained.

*****

"TIME TO GET RID of the extra baggage," Hopewell said as he unwound the chain from around the doors. "You get rid of Edna, and I'll dispose of Beanie. We'll take Marjorie with us. As soon as we get close to a phone, I'll call Kingpin and get us a new ride."

Later, PBJ would say that opening those truck doors was like unlocking the gates of hell.

Edna came at him like a wild woman, beating him with her cane until he was black and blue and sparkly. Some of the glitter even got in his eyes, blinding him to what was happening.

Beanie pelted Hopewell with containers of ice cream, knocking him down with a half-gallon of butter pecan. "Told you the nuts would add oompf," she announced triumphantly.

But Marjorie beat them both. Before Hopewell could get off

a shot, she pulled out Irene's pellet gun and hit him square in the knee. Truth be told, she was aiming for his head but, in her panic, missed the target a little. The shot to the knee was enough to keep him on the ground and gave the women a chance to wrestle the gun out of his hand.

"Looks like the 'girls' win this time, doesn't it?" Beanie remarked, holding the gun on the two men like she'd been catching criminals all her life. "You 'boys' stay right there on the ground until the police get here."

Beanie looked at her friends. "You called the police, right, Edna? You dialed 911?"

Edna shook her head. "Of course not. My cellphone doesn't work here, you know that. Marjorie, how about you?"

"Hey, I packed the heat, not a phone. Besides, mine doesn't work here either."

Hopewell smirked, "So you 'girls' think you're going to take us down and keep us here? How are you going to do that? Shoot me in the knee again?"

Beanie was infuriated. "We have everything we need to hold you until help arrives, Hopewell. Don't forget, I have your gun. And, yes, Marjorie will shoot your other knee if you so much as move a muscle. So, use your mouth for prayers instead of insults."

At just that moment, two pinpricks of light appeared down the road.

"Ladies, I believe the cavalry has arrived," Edna said, waves of relief in her voice.

The van stopped behind the ice cream truck, its headlights illuminating Hopewell and PBJ spread out on the ground. Stephen, Charlie, and Pearl jumped out of the van.

Beanie turned the gun over to Stephen and gave him a

hug. "I've never been so glad to see a physical therapist." She smiled at his companions. "Or a chef. Or a senior citizen with dementia."

Flashing blue lights and blaring sirens pierced the quiet night sky as two Palmetto police cruisers stopped in front of the ice cream truck.

Stephen handcuffed Hopewell and hauled him to his feet. "Let's go," he said. "Time for you to do a little song and dance about Kingpin. And you better not leave anything out. Your life is on the line."

"What about him?" Hopewell motioned his head toward the director. "Why does he get off scot-free?"

Stephen smiled. "He won't. I owe him big time for that hit in the back of the head. Was that really necessary, William?" Stephen rubbed his injury as he led Hopewell to the waiting police.

"Had to be believable, didn't I? Besides, I didn't hit you hard. You're just getting old." PBJ grinned.

Marjorie, Edna, and Beanie stared at each other in disbelief. Marjorie spoke first. "You mean to tell me that you were in on this all along?" She punched PBJ in the shoulder.

Beanie was next. "You let us believe you were taking us to Kingpin to be shot? You locked us in the back of that freezing truck? How could you?"

Edna was so angry she could hardly speak. "I should have hit you harder with my cane," was all she said. And with that, she knocked him a good one on his knee. Glitter flew everywhere.

"Hey!" the director protested, "I didn't let anything happen to you. And I'm black and blue from being beaten with that thing. I even got glitter in my eyes."

The director went on to explain. "As soon as I knew Marjorie was coming to Magnolia, I started using my contacts to get in with Kingpin's men. I told them I needed money, that an FBI pension wouldn't be enough for me to live comfortably, the way I wanted to.

"It didn't take long for me to be accepted into his organization. Apparently, dirty FBI operatives are a prized commodity for syndicates like Kingpin's. Unfortunately, Kingpin wasn't ready to trust me with everything right away. The good news was that he delayed taking Marjorie because he wanted to be sure he could trust me, and that took time. When Hopewell's poisoning scheme didn't work, he told Brett to stand down until he could bring me into the plan. Apparently, I was going to be the fall guy.

"I didn't know Hopewell was his man until this morning when the good 'pastor' knocked on my office door and introduced himself as Kingpin's hired killer. He told me all about his plans to take you, Marjorie. And I had to go with him to the shed to get Stephen out of the picture.

"So, you see? I really am a good guy. Remember, I gave you the flashlight."

Edna was ready to let him have another taste of her cane until Charlie reached over and took it from her. "Before you do any more damage," he said with a charming smile, "I better take this."

"Charlie?" Edna gaped at the man she thought she knew as Charlie Richardson. "What's going on?"

"I'm a retired Marshal. Stephen and I were partners back in the day, and he asked me to come help him with this case. I don't really have dementia. It was part of my cover. It allowed me access to all kinds of information I wouldn't have been able to get otherwise. People don't pay attention to you if they think you don't understand what they're saying."

Edna smiled at him. "Well, you were very clever, Charlie. You certainly had me convinced." Edna hugged him. "Thanks for coming to our rescue."

"Not exactly a knight in shining armor riding a white horse," Charlie laughed, looking down at his clothes. "Got my plaids and stripes mixed up, and I'm wearing two different shoes. All part of the act. And this," he patted the van, "is hardly a magnificent steed!"

When Charlie smiled at her, Edna's heart did a little flutter.

Now it was Pearl's turn to confess. She handed the gun over to the director, and with her head bent low, she told him everything, beginning with the stolen drugs. She was so ashamed of what she'd done. He'd trusted her for years, and she'd destroyed that trust in just one night.

"I know it was wrong, Director, and 'sorry' doesn't even begin to tell you how I feel. I did a terrible thing, stealing the drugs, and working with Hopewell. I even brought him the chemicals he used to try to kill Miss Marjorie. He told me he needed the stuff to get rid of some mice he'd seen in his apartment. I had some rat poison in the garage at home, and I was real glad to get rid of it.

"And then Miss Irene's cat died, and I heard it had been poisoned. I should have come to you right then and there. I know I should have. But I'd already started taking the drugs home to my mother. And I'm all she has. If I go to jail, who would take care of her?"

Big tears rolled down Pearl's face as she finally looked up at the director.

"I'm just so sorry."

"I know you are, Pearl. But we'll have to talk to the authorities about this. Maybe if you agree to share everything you have on Hopewell, they'll take that into consideration. We'll just have to see what happens." The director put his arms around Pearl, and she sobbed on his shoulder.

"Can you ever forgive me?" she asked.

"Yes, I forgive you. And we'll figure all this out together."

Then Pearl turned to Marjorie. "I never would have let him hurt you, Marjorie. I hope you can believe that. You, or Edna, or Beanie. That's why I'm here with Charlie and Stephen. I came to help them free you. I'm just sorry I didn't get a chance to shoot Hopewell. If ever a man deserved it..."

Pearl was interrupted by the putt, putt, putt of a golf cart motor. Two faint headlights were barely visible through the darkness. But then the driver of the cart let out a shout.

"Hey! Where's my ice cream?" yelled the delivery boy. As he drove closer, he saw the cartons of ice cream scattered on the road. Then he saw the gun in the director's hand, and in the dim cart light, his face turned as pale as French vanilla frozen yogurt.

"Is everybody OK? What in the world happened? Why is my butter pecan all over the ground?"

"We'll explain it some other time," said PBJ. "Right now, I'm going to drive the van back to the Manor. You can stay here if you want, and I'll call a wrecker to come help you with the truck."

"That's OK," the boy said. "This happens all the time, especially to new drivers who don't know the route real well. I'll just let some air out of the tires and be on my way. See you all next week." And he walked over to his truck, took out his pocket knife, and got to work on the tire valves.

"Time for us to head back to the Manor," said PBJ. "All

aboard."

But Marjorie couldn't move. All she wanted to do was stare up at the clear, dark skies and thank her lucky stars — or maybe God? — that Hopewell and Kingpin were out of her life for good.

Seventeen

Scattered, Smothered, and Covered

*R*ebecca was waiting for them in the dining room, nervously pacing back and forth in front of the windows. She nearly cried with relief when she saw the van pull into the parking lot. She flew out the door and greeted her grandmother with a huge hug that almost knocked the woman down.

"Nana, are you all right?" Rebecca held her at arm's length and surveyed Edna for blood, bruises, or broken bones.

"I'm fine, dear," Edna assured her. "Thanks to my trusty cane, that is. It really saved the day."

"What do you mean?" Rebecca was flabbergasted. "You were saved by your cane?"

Beanie piped up. "Well, that and Irene's pellet gun and a couple gallons of butter pecan ice cream."

Rebecca said, "I want to hear all about it, but right now, I'm just so thankful you're all OK. I made some coffee — although

I'm not sure how good it is — and there are leftover cookies from the talent show."

"You're a sweetheart. Come on inside, everybody, and we'll have a cookie," Edna said.

They walked into the dining room, where Rebecca had laid out the leftover cookies. The heavenly aroma of coffee filled the air.

Stephen spoke first. "A cup of coffee sounds great, Rebecca. But after that, Pearl and I have to ride down to the police station. Marjorie, you'll need to come, too. I'm sure you'll need to give a statement. We'll be late, so don't wait up for us."

"I'll go with you," said Charlie, downing his cup of coffee.

"Me, too," said PBJ. He jammed a chocolate chip cookie in his mouth and stuck a couple more in his jacket pocket before he followed the others out the door.

Beanie, Edna, and Rebecca watched out the windows as the men helped Pearl and Marjorie into the van.

"What's that all about?" Rebecca asked. "Is Pearl in some kind of trouble?"

"Well, Pearl's gotten herself in a pickle, that's for sure. But her actions tonight did a lot to make things right," said Beanie. "We'll just have to see what happens next."

"C'mon, Rebecca. Time to get you home. Beanie, do you want to ride along? I could use the company." Edna got up from the table.

Beanie said, "Sure. But all this talk about pecans has me in the mood for a pecan waffle. Maybe something scattered, smothered, and covered, too. What do you think, Rebecca?"

"Do you really need to ask?" the girl said with a grin.

A few minutes later, Beanie drove Edna's aging silver sedan into the parking lot of the Palmetto Waffle House. Most of her friends thought Edna's car was sporty for a woman of her age, but Edna referred to it as her "fat, white lady car with no spunk." She longed for the days when she drove her red Celica with four on the floor. Her worn-out knees had put an end to that era. She couldn't push in a clutch anymore. And trying to get in and out of that tiny car proved to be too much for any of her friends. But, oh, that car had been a showstopper.

When they arrived at the Waffle House, the trio grabbed a booth near the corner and settled in to study the menu.

"Good evening, ladies. Don't y'all look cute." The perky blonde waitress' name tag said 'Kathleen.'

"Have you been to the tractor pull over at the fairgrounds tonight? You'd fit right in with those outfits." The two women had almost forgotten they were still wearing their "Swingin'" costumes. Edna looked horrified, wishing she'd taken the time to shower and change. But true to form, Beanie just shrugged.

"Now, what can I get for you?" asked perky Kathleen, flipping her ponytail over her shoulder. Her makeup and hairdo were definitely made for a much younger person.

A fifty-year-old Taylor Swift, Edna thought. She winked at Beanie.

Beanie spoke to the waitress first. "A pecan waffle, heavy on the pecans, and a double order of hashbrowns, scattered, smothered, and covered. Oh, and a Diet Coke, please. I'm watching my figure."

Rebecca giggled at Beanie. Edna grimaced. "You eat all that, and you'll pay for it tomorrow."

"Humph. As we well know, after tonight's experience, tomorrow may never come. Eat, drink, and be merry is my new motto."

Edna shook her head and sighed.

Rebecca ordered a burger with fries, while Edna ordered eggs, toast, and decaf. "I'm so keyed up right now," Edna said, "I may never get to sleep. Any more caffeine and I won't sleep for a week."

Kathleen yelled their order over her shoulder to Dave, the cook. This was the old man's first night in the kitchen, and he'd already bungled a half-dozen orders.

"Tell me again what 'scattered, smothered, and covered' means?" Dave asked meekly. He was hunched over the grill, flattening out some burgers with a well-worn spatula. His shirt was covered with bacon grease, and his Waffle House paper hat was soaked with sweat. His thin gray hair hung limply over his ears, and his face was as red as the ketchup bottle on the counter.

Poor Dave had had a rough night.

Kathleen sighed and remarked to the ladies, "I've told him a hundred times already. Some people just aren't cut out for this kind of high-pressure work, you know?"

She went behind the counter to help Dave make the hashbrowns, then headed to the other end of the restaurant to take some more orders.

"All right, you two. Time to fess up. I want to know what went on tonight, and don't leave a single thing out." Rebecca was as serious as her grandmother had ever seen her. Edna decided to tell her the truth.

"OK, here goes," said Edna. "But hang on. It's quite a story."

She started the tale by sharing Marjorie's experience in the Philadelphia elevator. Beanie chimed in every now and then with details Marjorie forgot.

Perky Kathleen brought their food — Beanie's hashbrowns were perfect — and the women continued to eat and talk.

By the time they'd finished their food and their story, Rebecca was flabbergasted. "I can't believe you two pulled this off. You're my heroes," she said proudly. Then she looked at her grandmother. "But don't you ever do anything like that again!"

Beanie paid the bill and followed Rebecca and Edna out the door, but not before she complimented Dave on his hashbrowns. "Best scattered, smothered, and covered I ever ate," she exclaimed loudly enough for perky Kathleen to hear.

Dave smiled and waved. "Glad you liked them. Come back and see me!"

Hmmm. Nice smile. Pretty brown eyes. And a man that can cook. Well, sort of. Maybe I will pay you another visit, Dave.

Beanie shot him her best 'come hither' smile as she swayed and sauntered out the door.

"What are you doing?" Edna asked as Beanie climbed into the driver's seat. "You're going to break a hip for sure if you keep that up. Haven't seen that much motion from you since the last time there was a spider in your shower."

"Just trying to whet Dave's appetite for something a little spicier than soggy waffles. Looks like it worked, too." Through the restaurant window, Dave gave her a little wave and a big smile.

"Oh, good grief." Edna was beside herself. "Let's get poor Rebecca home before you corrupt her morals."

"On it!" replied Beanie as she whipped the car out of its parking space and headed onto the main road.

"Watch it, Danika." Edna cautioned her friend. "No speeding in this little town. Remember?"

"You don't need to worry about my driving, do we? I'm not the one that...."

Edna cut Beanie off. "Be quiet, Beanie. Rebecca doesn't know."

Rebecca piped up. "Doesn't know what, Nana? What don't I know?"

Beanie wasn't about to let her friend off the hook. "Rebecca has a right to know, Edna. She is your granddaughter, after all."

"Oh, all right," Edna gave in. "The reason I haven't been driving my car. And the cause of my hurt knee."

"What happened?" Rebecca was concerned.

"Well, I was backing out of a parking space at the Manor," Edna began. "And I accidentally ran into the director's golf cart. Did a little damage to the cart and my car."

"That's not so bad," Rebecca said, her voice sympathetic.

"Just wait, dear," Beanie chimed in, grinning. "The story gets better."

Edna gave Beanie a look that could have melted every gallon of butter pecan between Atlanta and Chattanooga. "When I realized what I'd done, I put the car in drive and hit the gas. A little too hard, you might say. I jumped the curb and ran right over the director's prize rose bushes."

"Oh, my," Rebecca said softly.

"There's more," Beanie could barely control herself.

"What happened next, Nana?"

"I hit the outside wall of the Manor and went crashing through a resident's window," Edna said, the color in her face rising.

"Ask her who's room she hit, Rebecca." Beanie was impatient for the punchline.

Edna said, "It was Irene Spencer's room. She'd been sound asleep, enjoying an afternoon nap in her rocking chair, and I came tearing through her window like a bat out of hell. Actually, it's a blessing I didn't hit her.

"But she attacked my car as if demons were after her. She picked up that old walker of hers and beat my windshield within an inch of its life. That's how her walker got all dented and her saddlebag went MIA.

"So, you can see how I might not be Irene's favorite, or PBJ's for that matter. And on top of all that, I hurt my knee and had to have surgery."

Rebecca had been silent for the last part of the story. But her face finally broke into a smile when she pictured Irene attacking her Nana's car.

"I'm sorry you hurt your knee, Nana," she said softly. "But I bet Irene was a sight to see. I bet she was mad as a hornet."

Beanie and Edna laughed. The car stopped in Rebecca's driveway, but before she got out, she leaned forward in her seat. "Nana, would it be all right if we said a prayer, thanking God for keeping you all safe tonight? And we need to ask Him to help Pearl and Marjorie, too."

"Sure, sweetheart." The three believers joined hands and prayed together. Then, Rebecca got out of the car and went to the driver's side window. She gave her Nana a kiss. "I hope I'm just like you when I'm elderly," she said, grinning.

"You two have the best adventures. See you in the morning!"

Beanie and Edna watched Rebecca go up the steps to her front door. "Do you suppose a Nana has ever loved a granddaughter as much as I love that child?" asked Edna.

Beanie wiped a tear from her eye. "She's a special one, that's for sure. It's a privilege to be a part of her life." She squeezed Edna's hand. "Now, let's get home. This country bumpkin Cinderella needs a shower and a good night's sleep. And I think the clock has already struck midnight."

Beanie carefully backed her car down the driveway and headed back to the Manor. What a day it had been.

And what a glorious day tomorrow would be.

MAGNOLIA
MANOR

Eighteen

Edna's Hallelujah Day

Sunday morning sunshine streamed through Marjorie's window. She woke slowly, unable to put her finger on why she felt so light, so free, until her brain kicked into gear, and she remembered. All of it. Hopewell and his threats, Kingpin and his crimes. Pearl's confession. She didn't have to live in fear anymore. She was finally safe.

She threw back the covers and was surprised by how stiff and painful her muscles were. Well, she mused, it had been quite a battle last night. She smiled at the thought. Edna, Beanie, and her, all working together to fight for good. Like a story from a comic book. Bet Wonder Woman never felt this sore.

She took a quick shower, thinking the warm water might help loosen her up. She fixed her hair, applied a little makeup, and put on a dress that WITSEC had packed in her bag for a special occasion. Sky blue with three-quarter sleeves and sleek silver buttons. There were even shoes to match.

She checked herself in the mirror, and pleased with what she saw, decided the WITSEC agent who put this outfit together might have a successful second career as a personal shopper.

She locked her room and headed down to the dining room for breakfast. Beanie and Edna had told her they'd meet her there this morning.

It felt strange there was no Stephen to talk to. He'd been her constant companion for months now, and suddenly he was gone. Off to protect other damsels in distress? She never expected to miss him, but surprisingly, she did.

Beanie and Edna were already at the table when she arrived. Beanie had chosen a lime green pantsuit for the occasion, and she looked spectacular. She'd even styled her hair and added a little makeup. Charlie Richardson had taken the extra place, sitting as close to Edna as he dared. He looked handsome this morning in a blue suit, white shirt, and snazzy tie. Edna beamed in a soft pink jacket dress with matching sandals.

Marjorie sat down in her chair and gratefully downed her coffee. Breakfast was quickly served, all the usual Sunday staples — eggs, bacon, biscuits, grits.

Marjorie was amazed at how hungry she was. Even the grits tasted good.

Charlie took Marjorie's hand. "It's all over, my dear. Hopewell gave up everything he knew about Kingpin, and the FBI picked him up from the Palmetto jail early this morning and transported him to the federal penitentiary in Atlanta.

You're safe, Marjorie."

"And I have all of you to thank," Marjorie said quietly. "Thanks for everything."

Beanie's mouth was full of grits, but that wasn't going to

keep her from talking. "We should track down criminals for a living. Nothing makes for restful slumber like capturing a couple of villains and saving the life of a good friend."

Marjorie smiled and squeezed her friend's hand. "And you, Edna? Did you sleep well? Any aches and pains?"

Edna grinned. "I'm fine, but I saw PBJ this morning, and he looks like he's been smacked around by an Atlanta linebacker, not a little old lady with a bedazzled cane." They all laughed.

Marjorie looked at Charlie. "Do you know what happened to Pearl?"

"The Manor doesn't want to press charges, but what she did could mean jail time for her. The judge did take into consideration her mother's condition. So, she was released into Stephen's custody for the time being."

"Stephen's still here?" Marjorie asked, just a little too much excitement in her voice.

"Why, yes, Marjorie," Charlie replied with a smile. "He'll be here until the trials are over. Maybe longer. Is that good news for you?"

Charlie, Edna, and Beanie all looked at Marjorie. Her face turned pink, and her eyes sparkled. "Well, yes, I think it is." Edna and Beanie clapped their hands in delight, and Charlie grinned.

"That's going to be great news for Stephen, too."

The four friends sat and talked and drank lots of coffee. Edna looked at her watch. "All right, everyone," said Edna. "It's time to go. It's almost ten o'clock, and the service starts at eleven."

They all got up from the table and walked toward the door. "Give me your keys, Edna." Charlie held out his hand to Edna. "I'll drive this morning."

"Now wait just a minute," Edna started to object, but then

she saw the look in his eyes. "I had a lot of time to talk to PBJ last night while we waited for Stephen and Pearl. He told me about your driving difficulties. I'd just feel a whole lot safer if I'm behind the wheel."

He held out his hand.

Knowing she was not going to win this argument, Edna dropped the car keys in his palm. "This isn't over," she said, a scowl on her face.

"I know," Charlie replied. His eyes twinkled. "Looking forward to the battle."

The sign outside the church said Morningside Christian Church. Charlie made a right turn into the gravel parking lot, and they all got out. Marjorie was surprised at the large number of cars filling the lot.

Edna rushed off to prepare for the baptism with Rebecca, who'd greeted her at the door. "C'mon, Nana. It's almost time!" Rebecca said as she pulled Edna down the aisle. They headed back to the changing rooms, where they'd put on white robes for the baptism.

Rebecca's excitement was contagious, and even Marjorie was touched by the girl's obvious joy.

"Would you like to take a closer look at the baptistery?" Beanie asked Marjorie, realizing the woman had probably never seen one like this before.

"Yes, I would," Marjorie answered shyly. She was familiar with the kind of baptismal font that sort of resembled a fancy birdbath. The kind she'd seen in the church she visited with Philadelphia friends at Christmas and Easter.

Beanie and Marjorie walked through a wooden door at the front of the church. They climbed a half dozen wooden steps, and when they got to the top, Marjorie could see down into the crystal-clear water. She wondered how many people over the years had found forgiveness and peace in that small, blue pool.

Would baptism do that for her?

Marjorie and Beanie took their places with Charlie in a pew near the front of the church. The congregation twittered and talked and laughed softly as they waited for the service to begin. How different from the total silence and formality she was used to in other churches she'd visited.

But what struck Marjorie the most was the simplicity of the church, the beautiful windows, the simple flowers on the plain altar. A stained-glass rendering of Jesus, his hands outstretched, glowing above the baptistery. The sunlight making the colored glass seem magical.

No, that's the wrong word. Not magical. Holy.

And then it was time. Marjorie watched as Edna, dressed in a white robe, walked carefully down the stairs into the waist-deep water. Her son, Rebecca's dad, held her arm to keep her steady.

Next came Rebecca, also dressed in white. She carefully climbed down the steps into the pool. Her mother helped her, making sure she didn't slip.

Edna stood behind her granddaughter. She took a dry handkerchief and held it over Rebecca's nose. Holding up her other hand toward heaven, Edna recited words that Marjorie knew had been repeated over and over in this little church and in churches just like it all over the world.

"Rebecca, I baptize you in the name of the Father, and of the Son, and of the Holy Spirit for the remission of your sins," Edna spoke in a clear, confident voice that gave Marjorie goosebumps.

Then she gently laid Rebecca on her back and lowered her all the way below the surface of the water.

When Rebecca came back up, there was no doubt something had changed. Even Marjorie could see the difference in the young girl. She glowed from the inside out.

Edna hugged and hugged Rebecca while tears flowed down both faces. And Marjorie knew she was witnessing something people rarely saw — true, complete, unconditional love.

As Rebecca climbed out of the water, the congregation smiled broadly and clapped their hands while the organist played a lovely old tune. A display of love and affection just to show Rebecca how much they cared about her and to rejoice with her in this blessed decision.

The outpouring of love touched Marjorie's heart.

She felt Beanie's hand touch hers. "Beautiful, isn't it?"

"Yes," she whispered, her eyes wet with tears. "Beanie? Do you think that…"

Beanie smiled at her. "Do you want to be baptized, Marjorie?"

Marjorie nodded. "I think so. Yes."

Beanie put her arm around her friend. "Well, here's all we need to know. Answer this question with a yes, and we're ready to go."

"It's that simple?"

"Yes, that's it." Beanie looked deep into her eyes. "Do you believe that Jesus is the Christ, the Son of the Living God, and your Savior?"

"Yes," said Marjorie, in a strong, confident voice she hadn't used in a long time. "I believe."

"Then let's do this!" Beanie pulled Marjorie out of the pew and down the aisle. "Wait, Edna! You get to stay wet a little longer!"

"What do you mean?" But then Edna broke into a huge smile and clapped her hands for joy when she saw Marjorie coming down the aisle with Beanie. "Marjorie, this is wonderful! Beanie and Rebecca can help you get changed into a robe. I'll be waiting right here. Oh, what a glorious day!" Edna exclaimed.

Beanie led Marjorie up the stairs to the changing room where Rebecca waited, her wet hair draped in a towel.

"Oh, Marjorie! This is awesome!" she said as she handed the older woman a white robe. "Whenever I think of the day I accepted Jesus as my Lord and Savior, I'll always remember you being right here with me. It's like we share a special birthday!" Rebecca grinned.

Marjorie smiled as she hugged Rebecca. "You're right. And I'll always think of you, too. Now I better change. I don't want Edna getting chilled in the water."

"Oh, you don't have to worry about that," Beanie said. "She'd wait there for you forever." She folded Marjorie's street clothes and put them on a stool. "But you're all set. Let's go."

Marjorie followed Beanie out the door of the changing room. Rebecca turned off the light and closed the door. The trio walked down the short narrow hall that led to the baptistery.

Edna greeted Marjorie with a big smile and open arms. "Come on in, my friend. The water's fine!"

Marjorie took Edna's hand and carefully climbed down the steps. She turned to face the congregation, smiling shyly.

Edna spoke to the congregation. "This is my dear friend, Marjorie Riley." Edna paused and smiled broadly at her friend. "I mean Sims, Marjorie Sims. She has come today to confess her faith in Jesus as her Lord and Savior, and she's asked to be baptized." Then she turned to Marjorie. "Are you ready?" she whispered.

Marjorie nodded.

Edna raised her arm and spoke in her strong, clear voice.

"Marjorie, I baptize you in the name of the Father, and of the Son, and of the Holy Spirit for the remission of your sins."

Then she lowered Marjorie down into the water just like she did with Rebecca. When Edna brought her up, Marjorie beamed.

"I'm so happy for you, Marjorie," Edna said. They stood in the water and hugged a little longer.

"Oh, but Edna, I have so many questions, so much to learn. Where do I start?"

"You've already started. Right here. Now, just let Jesus lead you a day at a time. He'll guide you as you go. And remember, you won't need any more mulligans. Ever."

Marjorie smiled. She knew this was more than just a mulligan. This was the start of a brand-new life. A life with purpose and meaning. And she knew, without a doubt, that she wasn't alone anymore.

MAGNOLIA MANOR

Nineteen

A New Mystery?

When Marjorie got back to her room at the Manor that afternoon, she found a note on her door from Stephen.

"Meet me at the director's office at three o'clock. Bring Beanie and Edna."

Marjorie looked at her watch. Half-past two. She quickly changed into a pair of linen capris and a light blue sweater, slipped into sandals, and pulled her hair into a ponytail. A quick check in the mirror, and she was out the door to find Beanie and Edna.

She bumped into the pair coming down the hall.

"Wonder what this is all about?" Edna said as she re-read the note. "Hope it's good news."

Marjorie knocked lightly on the director's door when they got to his office.

"Come in," answered the director.

Stephen and Pearl sat facing the director, who was seated behind his desk. Stephen looked weary and rumpled, obviously having gotten very little sleep. Dark circles showed under his eyes. Pearl looked even worse. Disheveled and nervous, her eyes flitted from person to person. She wrung her hands nervously and couldn't seem to sit still.

Three more chairs had been placed across from the desk to form a semi-circle. Marjorie, Beanie, and Edna sat down.

That old expression about cutting tension with a knife described the atmosphere in the office to a tee. PBJ finally spoke.

"Thanks for coming, ladies. Since you were directly involved with this matter concerning Brett Hopewell, we wanted to include you in the decision about Pearl's future here at Magnolia."

He cleared his throat before continuing. "The district attorney's office has decided not to file charges against her because of her clean record to date. And she is her mother's sole caregiver. However, Magnolia's Board of Directors wants to make an example of her to the rest of the staff. So, the D.A. recommended six months of community service, and the board agreed."

This news seemed to soothe Pearl's nerves. She inhaled deeply.

PBJ took a painfully long swallow of coffee. Everyone else fidgeted in their seats, waiting. Finally, Beanie couldn't take it anymore.

"So, what's the bottom line? What's going to happen to Pearl?" she almost shrieked at the director.

"We've decided that Pearl's loyalty to the Manor's residents means a lot. She's been more than a cook; she's been a friend to many of the folks who live here. She'll be allowed to continue here as the chef, but her movements will be restricted to the kitchen area only."

PBJ spoke in his most serious tone to Pearl. "If you are found in any of the nursing areas where meds are being stored, you'll be arrested on the spot. Understood?"

Pearl nodded. "Thank you, Director. I will not let you down again."

PBJ smiled. "I know you won't, Pearl. But there's more. We understand that taking care of your mother — Velma, isn't it? — has become quite a burden for you. We'd like to share that burden.

"As soon as Marjorie's apartment is ready for her to move back in — if that's what you'd like to do, Marjorie — we plan to move Miss Velma into that room, right between Edna and Beanie. At a very reduced charge that you can afford. And that's where you ladies come in." He spoke directly to the two women.

"Velma has certain challenges that will require extra attention. Our nursing staff will be able to provide most of what she needs, but she'll also need help with things like socializing and dressing. Oh, and learning to dance with the Raisin' Canes, of course."

Edna spoke up. "We can take care of that, Director. She's got to be better than Marjorie!"

"Hey!" Marjorie began to protest but then realized Edna was right. She smiled. "Well, I guess that's the truth. But I'm getting better. And, yes, I'd love to stay at the Manor."

Beanie put her arm around her. "You did just great last night. All it took was a bad guy with a gun to your head to turn you into a regular dancing queen!" Everyone laughed except Pearl. "So, it's settled, then?" she asked hesitantly. "Mama's going to move into the Manor, and I get to keep my job?" She turned hopeful eyes on the director.

"Yes, Pearl," he replied. "As long as you stick to our rules and complete your community service, you can put Hopewell and Kingpin behind you."

Pearl's smile lit up the room.

"Hey, everybody!" Charlie Richardson appeared at the office door. "I figured you'd all be in here. Everything worked out?" He directed his question at the director.

"Everything's just fine, Charlie," PBJ answered.

"Well, I was looking for someone to head to the Waffle House with me for a little supper. Since the cook's sitting right here and the kitchen staff is laying out bologna and white bread on the tables, I figured it'd be cold sandwiches for dinner tonight. But I'm craving something scattered, smothered, and covered."

Edna smiled at Charlie. "I'm in. How about you, Marjorie? Stephen? You, Director?"

"Sorry, guys, but I'm going to be tied up here tonight." PBJ stopped to consider what he'd just said. "Wait a minute. Maybe I shouldn't put it like that, considering all the excitement we've had in the past twenty-four hours. Let's just say I'm going to be pretty busy this evening. But could you bring me a piece of chocolate pie? That'll hit the spot."

"You bet, Director," Edna said. She turned to Stephen and Marjorie. "How about you two? Nothing quite as romantic as dinner at the Waffle House!"

Stephen grinned. "Not exactly what I had in mind for a first date, but what do you say, Marjorie?"

"Sounds good to me," she said and squeezed his hand.

Beanie was not about to be left out. "Well, I'm going, too. But you've got to give me a couple minutes to fix myself up. My favorite chef, Dave, might be manning the fryer tonight, and I want to look my best."

When the others laughed, Beanie spoke up. "Now, wait just a minute. Edna's found her man, Marjorie's found hers. It's my turn now."

"Beanie," the director interrupted her, "is that Dave Fisher from the Waffle House over on Highway 29?"

"Yes, that's him. Why?"

PBJ opened the local paper he had been reading before the meeting started.

"Seems like I just saw an article about him." He scanned the pages. "Yes, here it is. 'Waffle House employee David Fisher was arrested Saturday night by Palmetto police during a routine traffic stop. The officers involved say they discovered thousands of dollars worth of stolen electronics in the trunk of Fisher's car.'" He paused for a moment, skimming the rest of the page. "Oh, here we are. 'David Fisher was remanded to the Fulton County jail. No bond has been set.'"

All eyes turned to Beanie. "Oh, my," said Edna. "Don't think he's the right man for you, Beanie. Maybe you should keep looking."

Marjorie, Stephen, and Charlie nodded their agreement.

"There's something suspicious about this," Beanie said thoughtfully. "I think this situation deserves a second look. Besides, we've finished up Marjorie's case. Time to start on a new one.

"And between the three of us, you have to admit we have some pretty awesome detective skills!"

Marjorie and Edna nodded in agreement. "You know, the first thing we need to do is get over to Waffle House and talk to that waitress, Kathleen," Edna said. "I bet she knows something."

"She did seem like she was hiding something," agreed Marjorie.

Stephen and Charlie exchanged knowing looks. "I'll drive," said Charlie.

"I call shotgun," said Stephen.

"Not again," bemoaned PBJ, cradling his head in his hands. "All I wanted was a nice, quiet retirement job. And what do I get? More mayhem at the Manor. Geesh!"